June

ERLE STANLEY GARDNER

- Cited by the *Guinness Book of World Records* as the #1 bestselling writer of all time!

- Author of more than 150 clever, authentic, and sophisticated mystery novels!

- Creator of the amazing Perry Mason, the savvy Della Street, and dynamite detective Paul Drake!

- THE ONLY AUTHOR WHO OUTSELLS AGATHA CHRISTIE, HAROLD ROBBINS, BARBARA CARTLAND, AND LOUIS L'AMOUR *COMBINED*!

Why?

Because he writes the best, most fascinating whodunits of all!

You'll want to read every one of them,
from
BALLANTINE BOOKS

Also by Erle Stanley Gardner
Published by Ballantine Books:

THE CASE OF THE BORROWED BRUNETTE
THE CASE OF THE BURIED CLOCK
THE CASE OF THE FOOTLOOSE DOLL
THE CASE OF THE SHOPLIFTER'S SHOE
THE CASE OF THE FABULOUS FAKE
THE CASE OF THE CROOKED CANDLE
THE CASE OF THE HOWLING DOG
THE CASE OF THE MYTHICAL MONKEYS
THE CASE OF THE DEADLY TOY
THE CASE OF THE DUBIOUS BRIDEGROOM
THE CASE OF THE LONELY HEIRESS
THE CASE OF THE EMPTY TIN
THE CASE OF THE GLAMOROUS GHOST
THE CASE OF THE LAME CANARY
THE CASE OF THE CARETAKER'S CAT
THE CASE OF THE GILDED LILY
THE CASE OF THE ROLLING BONES
THE CASE OF THE SILENT PARTNER
THE CASE OF THE VELVET CLAWS
THE CASE OF THE BAITED HOOK
THE CASE OF THE COUNTERFEIT EYE
THE CASE OF THE PHANTOM FORTUNE
THE CASE OF THE WORRIED WAITRESS
THE CASE OF THE CALENDAR GIRL
THE CASE OF THE TERRIFIED TYPIST
THE CASE OF THE CAUTIOUS COQUETTE
THE CASE OF THE SPURIOUS SPINSTER
THE CASE OF THE DUPLICATE DAUGHTER
THE CASE OF THE STUTTERING BISHOP
THE CASE OF THE ICE-COLD HANDS
THE CASE OF THE MISCHIEVOUS DOLL
THE CASE OF THE DARING DECOY
THE CASE OF THE STEPDAUGHTER'S SECRET
THE CASE OF THE CURIOUS BRIDE
THE CASE OF THE CARELESS KITTEN
THE CASE OF THE LUCKY LOSER
THE CASE OF THE RUNAWAY CORPSE
THE CASE OF THE RELUCTANT MODEL
THE CASE OF THE WAYLAID WOLF
THE CASE OF THE MOTH-EATEN MINK
THE CASE OF THE LUCKY LEGS
THE CASE OF THE HALF-WAKENED WIFE
THE CASE OF THE DEMURE DEFENDANT
THE CASE OF THE SLEEPWALKER'S NIECE
THE CASE OF THE SULKY GIRL
THE CASE OF THE SINGING SKIRT
THE CASE OF THE SUBSTITUTE FACE
THE CASE OF THE NERVOUS ACCOMPLICE
THE CASE OF THE FUGITIVE NURSE
THE CASE OF THE GREEN-EYED SISTER
THE CASE OF THE HESITANT HOSTESS

The Case of the Angry Mourner

Erle Stanley Gardner

BALLANTINE BOOKS • NEW YORK

 Published in the United States of America by Ballantine Books, a division of Random House, Inc., New York, and simultaneously in Canada by Random House of Canada Limited, Toronto.

ISBN 0-345-37870-9

This edition published by arrangement with William Morrow & Company

Manufactured in the United States of America

First Ballantine Books Edition: October 1993

Foreword

A short time ago a man, driving along a Massachusetts highway at night, saw, or thought he saw, a car some distance ahead of him suddenly swerve off the road and vanish.

It was one of those fleeting impressions which might have been an illusion; but the driver was so strongly impressed he halted his car when he came to the point in question. He found that a grassy bank sloped down to a deep river.

He walked over to the bank of the river, and sure enough, deep down in the water he could see the red glow of the taillight on an automobile.

Officers were called, and, by the aid of grappling hooks, the automobile was raised to the surface. It was found to contain the body of one man, the driver.

Dr. Richard Ford, head of the Harvard School of Legal Medicine, and Medical Examiner for the Boston area, performed an autopsy. The cause of death was drowning and apparently there was no other contributing cause of death. There was no indication of heart trouble, or of any other acute condition which would have accounted for the man driving off the road. There were extraneous indications, however, that the driver might have been contemplating suicide particularly under such circumstances as to make it seem the death was due to an "accidental cause," thereby enabling his heirs to collect double indemnity.

Dr. Ford refused to accept the suicide theory, despite the fact that there was other circumstantial evidence indicating suicide and absolutely none to indicate death from any other cause. There was certainly no defect in the automobile's steering mechanism to account for the sudden plunge of the driver into eternity.

Proponents of the suicide theory strongly criticized Dr. Ford for his failure to so designate the cause of death.

However, as a true scientist, Dr. Ford is utterly indifferent to public praise on the one hand, or public criticism on the other. He only wants to satisfy his own conscience. What people may then say or think is of no concern.

So Dr. Ford pursued the even tenor of his ways.

Some six months later, another motorist driving along the same stretch of highway at night saw a car ahead of him at exactly the same place suddenly veer sharply to the right, plunge into the river and disappear.

Again the authorities were notified, and again grappling hooks brought to the surface a car in perfect mechanical condition, containing the body of a drowned driver who showed no cause of death other than drowning.

A thoroughgoing investigation was then launched and it was found that, due to a peculiar combination of circumstances, when an automobile headed in a crosswise direction took a short cut through the private driveway of a bottling works, an approaching motorist, seeing the glaring headlights, would naturally veer over to the right, thinking he was crowding the wrong side of the road. A slippery, grassy slope plunging abruptly into a deep river completed all the elements of tragedy.

As a result of Dr. Ford's personal investigation of the scene a guard fence was placed in an appropriate location and subsequent accidents have been prevented.

I think this case is a typical example of the work being done by Dr. Richard Ford.

If it can be said that there is an American intellectual aristocracy, Dr. Ford is certainly a member of that select group.

His father is one of the most thoroughly erudite men I have ever met. There is nothing stuffy about him. He is a practical, down-to-earth, lovable individual with more specialized knowledge at his fingertips than we expect any one brain capable of holding. His mother is a New England lady, and to those who know New England that is a comprehensive description.

Dr. Richard Ford is a scientist, a thinker, and one of the most expert pathologists in the country. His professional associates, when I asked them to comment on his character, emphasized the man's loyalty—a loyalty to his friends, to his profession and to his science.

It was my privilege to meet him at one of the seminars on homicide investigation conducted at Harvard Medical School under the auspices of Captain Frances G. Lee, that fabulous woman whose contributions to legal medicine and criminal investigation are now just beginning to bear the fruit of recognition, and which are destined to have a lasting effect.

To watch Dr. Ford perform an autopsy is a complete revelation. His hands, so deftly skillful they seem to be a part of his brain rather than of his body, move with a dexterity which is the quintessence of applied skill. He knows what to look for, where to look and how to appraise what he finds. He is beyond question one of the brightest minds in legal medicine today.

Personally, I think one of his most important contributions is the magnificent library of colored film he is compiling. He uses these colored slides on the occasions when he is called into consultation in various parts of the country.

If a prosecutor wants to know whether a wound of contact can produce a certain effect due to the expansion of gases, Dr. Ford can produce a formidable array of colored slides showing exactly the type of contact wound under discussion. If a man wants to know how much external and internal evidence will remain to indicate the wound of a small penetrating instrument such as an ice pick in various parts of the body, Dr. Ford can readily produce colored slides depicting every phase of such an injury.

These are the more common slides which can be appreciated by the layman. For the prosecutor who may want to know the appearance of certain changes in the cell structure of the kidneys due to the presence of bichloride of mercury, or whether it can be proven that cyanide of potassium was administered in the form of a capsule, Dr. Ford can produce slides showing the exact condition.

Books on legal medicine are not as a rule admissible in evidence, but slides showing typical conditions can usually be received in evidence, and as a result the importance of this library Dr. Ford is building up can hardly be overestimated.

In *The Case of the Angry Mourner* I deal with circumstantial evidence, which has a bad popular reputation, but which is nevertheless one of the most mathematically exact methods of proof known to the human mind.

Circumstantial evidence is infallible *if* it is all available. It is the interpretation of the circumstantial evidence which gives it its bad name.

This faulty interpretation is due in part to careless thinking on the part of investigative officers. It is also the result of the failure of unskilled officers to catalog and preserve *all* of the significant bits of circumstantial evidence.

All too frequently a detective at the scene of the crime jumps to a conclusion and then searches only for the evidence which will support that conclusion, consigning a really significant bit of worth-while evidence to oblivion.

Justice is founded upon evidence and evidence is founded upon fact. The work which is being done by Dr. Richard Ford is of such outstanding importance that I have written this foreword as a measure of my appreciation as a citizen, and am dedicating this book to him as a friend.

To

RICHARD FORD, M.D.
Acting head of School of Legal Medicine, Harvard University, Chief Medical Examiner Suffolk County, Massachusetts

Erle Stanley Gardner

Chapter 1

Belle Adrian wakened with an uneasy feeling that something was definitely wrong.

Light from a full moon streamed into the bedroom window, throwing a golden oblong on the rug, splashing across the foot of the bed. From the position of the shadows, Mrs. Adrian knew that it was long past midnight.

She turned and tried to compose herself and go back to sleep, but her thoughts kept turning to Carlotta.

In vain, her conscious mind argued with the apprehension which had suddenly gripped her. Carlotta was twenty-one, old enough to resent bitterly any attempt at maternal supervision; and Carlotta was either home in her bed or only a quarter of a mile away, at the cottage of Authur B. Cushing.

Mrs. Adrian fought back a desire to peek into Carlotta's bedroom. If Carlotta should happen to waken it would hurt her proud, young spirit to feel that she was being treated as a child—and yet—for more than three years now Belle Adrian had been fighting a battle with herself. The mother-protection attitude simply refused to be thrust aside.

Carlotta at seventeen had been obediently attentive; at nineteen good-naturedly tolerant; at twenty impatient.

Now at twenty-one Carlotta wanted it understood that her independence was a very real and definite thing. She had grown up. Her mother was a friend, a companion, but no longer a mentor or a chaperone.

Yet try as she might Belle Adrian simply could not wholeheartedly accept this changed concept. She might control the outward manifestations, but the inner feelings remained potent as ever. Carlotta at twenty-one was still her child, something to be protected.

Belle Adrian wondered exactly what time it was, whether Carlotta—a sudden inspiration gripped her. She could get the answer she wanted simply by looking in the garage.

She eased herself out of bed, slipped on a robe and soft slippers, tiptoed out of the back door and around to the driveway.

The door of the vacant garage was open. The interior loomed as a black, empty cavern.

Mrs. Adrian looked at her watch by the light of the moon. As she realized the lateness of the hour, anxiety gripped her and the black shadows of the empty garage took on added significance.

She walked slowly around the back of the house, toward the north side. From this point of vantage she could look across a cove in the lake to the cottage where Authur Cushing was spending the last week of his vacation. The broken ankle, which was keeping him confined to the house, was the result of a skiing accident which had occurred some ten days earlier when Carlotta and the wealthy young bachelor were racing neck and neck down the precipitous slopes of Bear Mountain. For this reason, Carlotta felt a certain responsibility and had of late been a frequent visitor at the Cushing cottage.

Now that Arthur Cushing was planning to return to the city, it was only natural that he should have invited Carlotta for dinner and a showing of the sixteen-millimeter colored movies, which had been sent to the city for processing and had returned only that afternoon.

Mrs. Adrian assured herself that after all, judged by present standards, the hour was not late. She tried to laugh off the mood that had wakened her, a very definite feeling of apprehension, which she hadn't been able to shake off.

The shimmering waters of the cold lake, glinting frostily in the moonlight, reflected lights from the windows of the Cushing cottage. These lights seemed warm and reassuring. Undoubtedly everything was all right, and any moment now the headlights of Carlotta's car would be probing their way through the darkness.

Mrs. Adrian shivered with cold and a nervous reaction. She was, she decided, going back to bed, and then she was going to sleep. After all, Carlotta was no longer a child. Belle Adrian would simply have to learn self-discipline, and . . .

Somewhere across the lake sounded the thin scream of a woman. It was weak with distance, yet, despite that fact, retained the overtones of pure terror. It was a long-drawn, high-pitched scream.

Mrs. Adrian waited only for a moment, to see if there was any repetition of that scream. Then she dashed to her bedroom, threw on a tweed skirt and jacket, and without even bothering to put on stockings, thrust her feet into the first available shoes, and dashed out of the house.

An arm of the lake lay between her and Cushing's cottage. By ignoring the road, and taking a trial along the margin of the lake, Belle Adrian could save an appreciable distance.

Cottages were springing up along the lake shore, at one time used only as farming land, but now gaining fame as a winter resort. Later on, when the lake had frozen solid, there would be ice skating and bonfires with huge pots of steaming coffee; now there was the skiing of early winter.

At this elevation of more than a mile above sea level, Mrs. Adrian found it difficult to maintain a rapid pace, but she forged ahead, determined that no matter what Carlotta might think, she was going to investigate that scream. It had seemed to come from the direction of Cushing's cottage, straight across the arm of the lake, the sound thinned by distance, yet alarmingly clear in the cold, windless night.

Frost had formed a white blanket under the moon. Frost-coated vegetation whipped against Belle Adrian's bare legs as she hurried along the narrow pathway. Breathlessly, she came to the Cushing cottage.

Dexter C. Cushing, the banker, maintained this cottage as a year-round recreation place, although Arthur, the son, used the house far more than his father. The building occupied a choice position on a jutting peninsula. A dock for the speedboat which was kept in service in summer cast a black shadow. There were barbecue grounds out at the water's edge, and a wide parking place in front of the garage on the north.

Belle Adrian noticed that draperies had been pulled across the front windows. Only the side windows were undraped. The lights inside the house threw golden oblongs on the half-frozen ground, and the shadows of the holly wreaths of the Christmas season were black ovals in the middle of these oblongs.

Mrs. Adrian ran up the stairs of the front porch and rang the bell. Then suddenly she was in the grip of a reaction. What story would she tell when the door opened? Should she mention the scream? What scream? How did she know it came from this cottage?

An image of what might happen formed in her mind. She could see Cushing's amused features as he listened, could see Carlotta's face over his shoulder, eyes blazing indignantly. Arthur Cushing might not notice the telltale state of her wardrobe, but Carlotta most certainly would.

The warmly lighted house was altogether too conventionally safe, too indicative of a modern man and woman forming a friendship in front of an open fire. The intrusion of a disheveled, anxious mother would be too hopelessly old-fashioned, too utterly ridiculous.

Belle Adrian took refuge in flight. She ran from the porch around the side of the house, toward the back, hugging the shadows closely, trusting that Arthur Cushing might explain the jangling doorbell as the prank of some prowler or perhaps a trick of his own ears.

For long seconds Mrs. Adrian crouched by the back of the house, waiting to hear steps that would answer the doorbell.

There were no steps.

Making swift reappraisal of the situation, she cautiously circled the house, looking for, and failing to find, Carlotta's automobile.

But she found an unexpected something which promptly restored all her fears, magnified her dread. The window on the north side of the house, at the back, was pouring light out into the yard. In the golden glow of that light she could see that hoarfrost had settled over the yard, giving the ground a cold, metallic glitter. But there was more than the frost which glittered. There were particles of glass reflecting light from the interior of the room and there were two long, black tracks through the white frost, made by the tires of an automobile which apparently had but recently been driven from the yard. The tire tracks started at the end of a dark oblong, the place were the parked car had kept frost from forming.

Cautiously, Mrs. Adrian tiptoed forward to investigate.

The pieces of glass lying on the ground were jagged slivers, coated with silver, apparently the fragments of a thick mirror which had been shattered against the side of the window casement.

The window itself had been broken and pieces of thin window glass were mingled with the thick, silvered fragments from the mirror.

From the ground, Mrs. Adrian could not see into that room, but the gaping hole in the fractured glass of the window, the silvered mirror fragments on the ground, told their own story, and in a sudden panic Mrs. Adrian called, "Is anything wrong?"

Her voice echoed back frostily.

She ran once more around the house to the front door, jabbed frantically at the bell button, tried the doorknob, rattling the door, then pounding with futile fists against the panels.

The latch of the spring lock on the inside held the door firmly closed.

Belle Adrian circled to the back door and, without pausing to knock, tried the knob. She hesitated only for a brief moment as the door swung open on well-oiled hinges.

"Carlotta!" she called. "Carlotta . . . Arthur . . . Mr. Cushing!"

When there was no answer, she moved through a kitchen, opening doors with a panic-stricken haste which gave place to frozen terror as she stood on the threshold of a room that evidently served both as den and bedroom.

There were skis, pennants and trophies, guns hanging on

pegs, swords and pistols, a collection of framed autographed photographs, a bed, and in the center of the room a wheel chair.

The floor around the wheel chair was littered with broken glass. A framed picture had been reduced to a crumpled wreckage and decorated a corner near the window.

In the wheel chair, slumped grotesquely in death, was Arthur B. Cushing. A trickle of red had formed a sinister stain on the man's silk shirt, a stain which welled down from a dark, round hole. There were spatters of red on the floor.

On the floor was a circular, glittering object which reflected the light. It was an open compact lying with shattered mirror and spilled powder almost at the feet of the dead man.

Belle Adrian knew that compact, even without noticing the engraving of the gold surface. It was a compact which Arthur Cushing had given Carlotta for her birthday.

For a space which seemed an eternity Belle Adrian stood looking at the inert, slack-jawed corpse in the wheel chair, at the broken window, at the broken compact.

Then she started to work.

As steadily and calmly as though she had been cleaning a kitchen after a meal, she set about removing every bit of evidence that would connect Carlotta with the death of Arthur Cushing.

Chapter 2

Sam Burris went methodically about the difficult task of waking his wife.

"Did you hear what I just heard?" he asked insistently.

She snored gently.

Sam Burris gripped her shoulders and shook her.

Always a heavy sleeper, his wife muttered unintelligible words. Sam shook her head again, and her eyes fluttered open.

"What is it?" she asked thickly.

"Didn't you hear all that noise?" Burris asked.

"No," she said, and promptly closed her eyes.

Burris shook her. "There's trouble of some sort. I heard glass breaking, and the sound of a shot."

Mrs. Burris, always eager for bits of gossip concerning the vacation colony around the lake, promptly started struggling to a sitting position. "Where'd it come from?"

"Sounded like it came from the Cushing cottage, and that's the only one where lights are on. I looked out the window but I couldn't see anyone moving around over there."

Mrs. Burris was wide-awake now. "Hand me that robe, Sam."

Sam, slender, wiry, active, handed his wife the heavy quilted robe from the foot of the bed, and then promptly huddled his spare frame into the warmth of the covers. Mrs. Burris donned the robe, and, accompanied by a squeaking of springs and a heaving of the mattress, dislodged herself from the bed. At that moment a woman screamed, a long-drawn piercing scream, quite evidently coming from the Cushing cottage.

"Those Cushings!" Burris grunted. "Wish't I'd never seen

'em.'' Having originally owned all the lake front, he had been tempted by the elder Cushing to sell some two hundred acres.

''Paid you your own price for it,'' his wife said tartly. ''It's your own fault if you didn't ask him more. What do you s'pose is going on over there?''

''Probably the same old thing,'' Burris said. ''How did I know he was planning a swank resort? I charged him four times what it was worth for farming.''

''And made a sucker of yourself doing it,'' she said. ''People have been laughing at you ever since. However, now he's a neighbor, so we might's well get along.''

''We don't have neighbors any more,'' Burris grumbled, ''just people who own adjoining property.''

''It's your own fault . . . Sam, I saw a light in that cabin across the lake where the woman and her daughter are living.''

''Mrs. Adrian?'' Burris asked, his voice losing its whine and taking on a note of sudden interest. ''The spyglass is up there over the window. Take a look.''

His wife took the spyglass from its shelf above the window. ''I wonder if the Adrians heard that scream.''

''Could be,'' Burris grumbled. ''It's cold. Come on back to bed.''

His wife placed the telescope to her eye, paying no attention to her husband's request. Once she was on the scent of a scandal no power on earth could have coaxed her away from window and spyglass.

''Certainly have great carryings-on around the lake these days,'' she snorted. ''That Cushing boy has women over there half the night. Courting certainly has changed since the time you used to row me around the lake in that green boat your dad had.''

''They don't call it courting now,'' Sam said. ''And the damn boat kept leaking,'' he snorted. ''I used to carry along a tomato can, and about the time I'd get interested in courtin', the danged water'd come sloshing in. . . . For heaven's sake, Betsy, come on back to bed.''

His wife ignored the request, remained seated at the window, telescope glued to her eye. Fifteen minutes went by. "Looks like there's a smashed window over there, Sam, and I think I saw someone move just now. Just what was it you heard?"

Sam Burris yawned, said sleepily, "Nothing much, I guess. It woke me up—sort of a smashing sound, maybe a shot or a car backfiring, then a car having trouble getting started."

Mrs. Burris, always a great talker, started a running fire of conversation. "Remember the time we went fishing in that old boat and the thunderstorm came up? We went in Mosby's old barn and you forgot to turn the boat bottom side up."

"I didn't forget," Burris protested sleepily. "It was just too danged heavy. I didn't think it was going to rain that hard."

"Well, it certainly rained," she said. "Sam, have you forgotten about that?"

Sam's reply was a gentle snore.

"Sam!" she called. "Sam! Wake up and look here!"

Sam Burris ceased snoring. "What's the matter?"

"You come here, Sam Burris."

At the peremptory tone in her voice Sam obediently rolled out of bed and went to the window.

"Look over there," she commanded.

Together, they stood looking across the three-hundred-foot gap which separated their bedroom from the lighted window of Arthur Cushing's house.

"Someone moving around all right," Sam said. "So what?"

Mrs. Burris again raised the telescope. "Belle Adrian, Carlotta's mother," she said. "You'd think a woman *her* age would have more sense than to be gallivanting around at this hour in a bachelor's apartment. Can you imagine that? Arthur Cushing's been going with Carlotta, and now the mother . . ."

Sam Burris abruptly reached for the telescope. "Hey," he said, "are you sure?"

His wife pushed his hand aside. "Of course I'm sure. Think I can't recognize her? I can see her just as plain as day. . . . There's a window broken all right. . . . I don't see anyone else in there. She keeps moving around and . . ."

Sam Burris unceremoniously grabbed the telescope from his wife's hands.

"Sam Burris," she exclaimed, all but speechless, "what do you mean, grabbing things like that and . . ."

There was a sudden, new, crisp note of authority in her husband's voice. "Shut up," he said, "this may be serious! Let *me* see."

"Well, I like that! Grabbing things out of a body's hand like that! Who do you think you are?"

Burris didn't answer her, other than by reporting what he was watching. "You were right. I didn't think it was possible, but darned if you didn't call the turn!"

That mollified her. "Of course I was right. I guess my eyes are as keen as they ever were. What's happening?"

"It's the Adrian woman—the mother—moving around like she's picking things up. . . . How do you suppose that window got broken? . . . Can't see anything of Arthur Cushing. He doesn't seem to be around and . . . Say, I'd better go over there and see if everything's all right. . . . What time is it, anyway?"

"How would I know? The clock's in the kitchen. Go take a look at it if you want to."

"Can't you look? I'm busy watching."

"You look and I'll watch."

Sam Burris surrendered the telescope. "I s'pose we should do something about this. Maybe there's been an accident." He started dressing.

"Perhaps one of these girls gave him what he had coming," Mrs. Burris suggested.

"It's about time."

"Don't talk like that, Sam. You going over?"

"Reckon I ought to."

"Cushing won't like it."

"Never mind what he likes. That broken window and the woman screaming . . ."

"It was Belle Adrian who screamed, Sam."

"How do you know?"

"Well—it just had to be. . . . Sam, the way she's doing things you can just tell she's being sneaky about it all."

"Nope, I think the daughter screamed and she's trying to cover up."

"You go see what time it is. I want to know."

He took a hand flashlight, crossed through the dining room to the kitchen, returned and said, "It's half past two. I'm going over."

"I guess you'd better."

"Don't say anything about this Adrian woman being over there."

"And why not, I'd like to know?"

"Because they're nice people. Her daughter was over there earlier and if there's been a little trouble . . . Well, you talk a lot."

"Well, I like that! Who are you to give orders? I guess if that woman's gallivanting around over there with a man ten years younger than she is—trying to beat her daughter's time, I've got a right to comment on it after I've seen it with my own eyes."

"You just keep quiet," he said. "Gossip gets around here too fast the way it is."

"Sam Burris, do you have any idea who you're talking to or what you're saying?"

"These Adrians are nice people," he insisted doggedly.

"But, Sam, you said you heard a shot."

"I heard a backfire. If there'd really been a shot do you think Mrs. Adrian would be moving around there so casual-like?"

"It isn't casual, Sam Burris, and if her daughter had been over there with Arthur Cushing, knowing what we know about him . . ."

"Well let's give 'em both a break. With what we know

about Arthur Cushing we know it's about time *somebody* did something."

"You go see what's happened, Sam. It may be she just caught him trying his cave-man stuff with her daughter and it may have been something real bad that happened."

With obvious reluctance, Sam Burris went to the closet, put on a heavy coat, cap and ear muffs.

"You can quit stalling around now, Sam," Mrs. Burris said acidly. "She's gone."

Chapter 3

Mrs. Adrian, her heart still pounding with the excitement incident to the events of the past hour, came to the point where the trail joined the road and then turned into her own yard.

The garage was still empty.

For a moment she was puzzled by this, since she had felt Carlotta must have left the Cushing cottage very shortly after that terrified scream had knifed through the cold silence of the night. Normally she would have put the car in the garage, closed the garage door, and gone to bed.

Now the yawning emptiness of the garage could mean but one thing—Carlotta had taken refuge in flight—the most utterly insane, foolish thing she could possibly have done.

Flight was evidence of guilt. Flight would inevitably point the finger of suspicion directly toward Carlotta. The police would learn that Arthur Cushing had had a dinner date with Carlotta, would seek to check with Carlotta, and, finding her gone, would immediately regard her as Suspect Number One. After that even the shrewdest lawyer would never be able to concoct a story of what had happened that would be acceptable to a jury.

Mrs. Adrian paused only long enough to take a swift stock of the situation. Carlotta's flight must be covered up, changed into a normal action that had been planned several days ahead—a trip to the city for shopping purposes.

That meant Mrs. Adrian must do two things. She must find Carlotta before the police started looking for Arthur Cushing's dinner guest, and she must get Carlotta's suitcase packed. At least an overnight bag that would rob Carlotta's hurried departure of the stigma of a flight.

Mrs. Adrian burst into Carlotta's bedroom, dashed toward the closet, then suddenly stopped, rigid with surprise, as she saw motion in the shaft of moonlight which fell across Carlotta's bed.

Carlotta started to scream, then caught herself as she recognized her mother.

"Why, Mumsey! Whatever in the *world* is the matter?" Carlotta asked.

"You!" Mrs. Adrian exclaimed.

Fully awake now, Carlotta said quietly, "Naturally. Whom did you expect?"

"I . . . how long have you been home?"

"Heavens, I don't know. Quite a while. Why?"

"The car isn't in the garage."

"I had a puncture halfway home, so I left it and walked the rest of the way. Now, for heaven's sake, don't tell me you've been worrying, prowling around, and . . ."

"Carlotta, I wasn't snooping."

"I didn't say snooping, Mother, I said prowling."

"Well, it means the same thing."

Carlotta said easily, "Don't be old-fashioned, Mumsey, and don't get on the defensive. After all, I suppose it's hard for a mother to realize her child has grown up."

Mrs. Adrian switched on the lights.

"Did you . . . Did you have any trouble, Carlotta?"

"Let's not go into it now, dear, please."

Mrs. Adrian walked over to the chair where Carlotta had tossed the vivid-colored blouse she had been wearing. Mrs. Adrian picked it up off the chair and examined a jagged rip in the cloth at the front of the blouse.

Carlotta flushed. "Now, Mumsey, you *are* snooping!"

"Carlotta, I'm . . . I *must* know what happened."

Carlotta said indignantly, "All right, Mumsey, you've asked for it. I've grown up. I have curves. Men notice them. They like to make passes. It's their nature. I'm afraid we're not going to be able to change their nature. The fact that the blouse is torn should convey its own answer. Your maternal concern would be much more appropriate if the blouse had *not* been torn."

"It isn't that, Carlotta. I want to know what . . . what did you *do*?"

Carlotta said wearily, "I told him 'no' gently for the first four or five times, then I showed him I meant business, and when he put his weight behind a forward pass I swung on him hard—and came home."

"You slapped him?"

"Slapped him, hell!" Carlotta said. "I gave him the palm of my hand right on the point of his jaw. Frankly, I don't mind men making passes. I like it. I also like men who can appreciate the meaning of a negative. Now, if you've pried enough into my private affairs, suppose we separate for a while and go through the motions of getting some sleep, although I don't suppose I'll be able to—now."

Mrs. Adrian reached into the pocket of her tweed coat, said calmly, "Here's the broken compact you left behind you, Carlotta."

Carlotta's bare legs flashed as she tossed back the covers and flung herself out of bed, reaching for a robe as she came to her feet.

"*Where* did you get that?"

"Over at Arthur Cushing's cottage."

Carlotta's face drained itself of expression. "You—good heavens, Mother, you haven't been *there*?"

Mrs. Adrian nodded.

Carlotta, tight-lipped, said, "I'm sorry, but that's going just too damned far, even for a mother."

"And," Mrs. Adrian went on, "I found him sitting in the wheel chair, a bullet hole in his chest, your compact on the floor, and a window smashed where . . ."

"A bullet hole!"

"Yes."

"You mean that he's . . . ?"

"Yes, dead."

"And what did *you* do?"

"I removed all of the evidence that would indicate you had been there, Carlotta, at least I *hope* I did."

"Oh, my gosh!" Carlotta exclaimed. "Get these lights out," she commanded. "Let's not let the whole community know we're up. Crawl into bed and let's talk this thing over."

Chapter 4

Cold, frosty daylight was a gray mantle on the lake. The first faint color in the sky silhouetted the jagged mountains against a metallic, greenish-blue backdrop.

The doorbell of the Adrian cottage suddenly rang long and shrill.

Inside the cottage, Mrs. Adrian held the flashlight so that the fingers of her left hand covered the lens. The first two fingers were spread slightly apart so that a small, almost imperceptible slit of light furnished the illumination by which she and Carlotta surveyed each other's dismayed faces.

"This will be the law, Carlotta," her mother whispered. "I thought . . . I hoped we'd have time to get you packed up and on your way. Oh, why couldn't we have had a break?"

"Darn that puncture," Carlotta answered. "If it hadn't been for that . . ."

"Remember now," Mrs. Adrian interrupted, "you quarreled with Arthur almost immediately after the servant left. You came home and left him sitting in the wheel chair. He didn't even go to the door with you. He was mad and sullen. You drove away and had the puncture on the road home. Then you left the car and walked home. You had been planning to visit . . ."

"But, Mumsey," Carlotta interrupted, "they've here now. Won't it be better to pretend I hadn't been planning to go anywhere?"

"You forget the packed suitcases, darling."

"Let's put them in a closet."

"They might search."

The bell kept up its steady, insistent ringing.

"If only we can keep Harvey from hearing about this," Carlotta whispered.

"But he's a lawyer, dear. He might help."

"I don't want help at that price, Mumsey. Harvey's intentions are honorable, but remote. I love him. Arthur Cushing was a playboy. *His* intentions were dishonorable and immediate. I suppose I liked to play with fire. . . . You'll have to get out of your clothes, Mumsey. We can't just go on ignoring that confounded doorbell."

Belle Adrian slipped out of her shoes, moved cautiously in bare feet. "Get into bed, darling," she said, and then called in a voice she tried to make thick with sleep, "Who is it?"

The only answer was the insistent, intermittent ringing of the doorbell.

"Just a moment," Belle Adrian called wearily. "Let me slip on something."

She stood near the bed hastily stripping off her garments, then she threw a robe about her and went to the door to switch on the porch light.

She saw Sam Burris standing patiently in the light of the porch, his ears and nose red with the cold.

Mrs. Adrian opened the door, yawning, and said, "Why . . . Why, it's Mr. Burris! What is it? What's the trouble?"

"I want to talk with you," Sam said.

"But at *this* hour of the morning . . ."

"It's important."

"Well, for heaven's sake! Things are a mess here but come in. We can go in the front room. You'll have to wait there until I dress."

Sam Burris seemed apologetically ill at ease as he seated himself on the chair Mrs. Adrian had indicated.

"Well, what is it?" she asked.

"I don't hardly know how to begin," he said, his eyes on the floor.

"Well, after all, Mr. Burris, at this hour of the morning I must assume that it's terribly important and . . ."

"It is. You know we have the cabin up there where . . ."

"I know where your cabin is, yes."

"And our bedroom window is so we can look right down into Arthur Cushing's den in the Cushing cottage."

"Look right *into* his den," she exclaimed. "Why, you must be a city block away. You . . ."

"That's right, ma'am, just about a hundred yards. But you can see quite plain at night, looking into a lighted room when the shades ain't down, and sounds are good and distinct at night."

"Just what are you getting at?"

He said, "Arthur Cushing . . . Well, I wouldn't want a daughter of mine around much with Arthur Cushing."

"Well, thank you very much," Mrs. Adrian said tartly, "but in the first place daughters these days are inclined to live their own lives, and in the second place I certainly don't appreciate being wakened from a sound sleep to be warned about my daughter's friends, which I suppose is what you're trying to get at."

"Well, ma'am, it's more than that. You see, Arthur Cushing is dead."

"Dead!" she exclaimed. "Dead! Arthur Cushing is dead?"

He nodded.

She could for the moment think of nothing to say, but watched him with anxious eyes, wondering just how much he knew, knowing that she must encourage him to a point where she had drained him dry of information, yet doing it in such a skillful way he would have no idea that he was being pumped and definitely no realization of her keen interest.

"Well," she said at length, "that is exceedingly tragic. It must have been rather sudden. My daughter, I believe, had dinner with him last night. They were looking over some motion pictures, and because of Arthur Cushing's leg they didn't go out. She came home early and . . ."

"You don't need to explain things to me, ma'am. That's what I'm trying to tell you."

"Perhaps," she said, "you'd better go ahead and tell me. Don't be embarrassed; speak right up, Mr. Burris. What is it?"

He said, "Arthur Cushing liked to be the rich gentleman when he could get what he wanted that way, but when he couldn't he had a little terrible temper and . . . Well, he'd get rough."

Mrs. Adrian, by rigid self-control, sat perfectly still, saying nothing.

"My wife and I have seen lots of things over there," Sam Burris went on. "We'd hear angry voices; sometimes we'd hear a woman scream, and . . . Well, Arthur never bothered to pull that shade on the window of his den. He evidently felt that nobody could see anything at that distance."

Again Mrs. Adrian said nothing.

"But," Sam Burris went on, "you see, we've been around the lake for quite a while and have a pretty good telescope, thirty power, and it's plenty clear."

"A telescope!" Mrs. Adrian echoed, trying to keep the dismay from her voice.

He nodded, then after a moment said, "I don't want you to think we're snoopers or what they call Peeping Toms or anything, but after all, when you hear a woman scream along late at night and look out of the window and see two people struggling, you have to be sure that everything's all right before you can go back to bed."

She nodded, tight-lipped.

"I'm a very light sleeper," Sam Burris said. "My wife sleeps awful heavy. You have to pound her to get her awake when she gets to sleep. She's like lots of the women around here. They do a right smart lot of talking, so I don't tell her *all* the things I see.

"First time anything like that happened I woke her up and she thought for a while we should interfere, then it turned out there wasn't any need to interfere."

"What do you mean by that?"

"That girl was plenty able to take care of herself," Sam

Burris said. "Believe me, she certainly swung on him, and then she walked out."

"That was . . . some time ago?" she asked.

"Two or three months."

"Oh," she said, and then frowned with annoyance at herself for letting the note of relief be so obviously audible.

"Then the second time," Burris went on, "it was just the other way."

"What do you mean?"

"Well, this girl kept putting up a fight. I got dressed. We don't have any telephone and I was going out to get the sheriff and then . . . Well, she seemed to like it. The first thing we knew, they were kissing each other right up there in front of the window—sort of made me sick to think that girls would fall for things like that."

"Some women do," Mrs. Adrian said. "Perhaps she was putting on an act. Did you . . . Did you recognize her?"

"Could see her plain as day through the telescope," Burris said. "She's been back quite a few times since. A mighty good-looking girl. I don't know her name. Sort of black hair and slate-colored eyes . . . but . . . Well, I don't want you to think we deliberately spy on people . . . I just don't like to have people like Arthur Cushing here in the neighborhood."

"You brought him in here, didn't you. . . . That is, pardon me, I mean you sold him the land."

"I made a fool of myself," Burris admitted. "I was sure dumb. They had a real estate man hunt me up and tell me all sorts of lies. This real estate fellow told me he had a man who wanted to get some farming land; didn't want too big crops but wanted a farm that he could lose money on, so he could make a deduction on his income tax.

"Well, I thought if he wanted to lose money I'd just accommodate him, so I set a price on a couple of hundred acres that was about four times what it was worth, and then agreed to give an option on the rest of my property at about four times what it was worth—for farming land."

"And then it turned out that the purchaser was Dexter Cushing who was negotiating for the land?"

"That's right. He didn't want it for farming. He wanted it for a resort hotel. . . . I guess it was Arthur who put the bee in his bonnet. Anyway, they built that cottage over there and then announced their plans for this big resort hotel, and of course that's put me in a spot."

"But won't your land increase in value?"

"For tax purposes," Burris said, "I'm stuck with the taxes; they got their option to buy any time they get good and ready. But let's not waste time with all that. You said I brought them here. I just want you to know what really happened. Now what I want to get at is that we saw you over there tonight."

Mrs. Adrian sat perfectly upright and rigid in the chair. "Saw *me*?" she asked, with what she hoped was just the right amount of frigid incredulity in her voice.

"Now, ma'am, please don't get me wrong," Sam Burris pleaded. "We . . . Well, we know you're awful nice people. You and your daughter, Carlotta, are just the nicest people we've had come in here."

"Thank you," she said icily.

"And . . . Well, I knew what was going to happen, that is, I knew what Arthur Cushing was going to try and . . . Well, I thought some of coming over to you and telling you a few things—made up my mind I'd do it if there ever was any need to."

"That was very nice of you, but I still don't understand what you mean by saying you saw *me* over at the Cushing cottage. Carlotta was there, of course, and . . ."

"We saw Carlotta," Sam Burris said, "and after we went to bed . . . Well, I was the one who wakened first, when I heard the glass breaking and the shot, and then a woman screamed and . . . Well, we got up to see what had happened."

"If there is anything wrong," she said, "it is your duty to go to the officers and . . ."

"I've been to the officers," he explained patiently. "That's why I couldn't get over here any sooner."

"Oh," she said weakly.

"Now if you'll just listen, ma'am, and let me explain. We may not have much time and I'd like to have you understand."

"Very well," she said, "go ahead and explain."

"It ain't easy for a man like me to talk to a woman like you and tell her what I have to say," Burris blurted, "but I know what you're up against. Your daughter killed Arthur Cushing, and he certainly had it coming. You heard her scream and heard the shot and went over to find out what it was all about. Then you helped your daughter cover up. Now, of course, I don't know what evidence the sheriff can get, but as far as my wife and me are concerned, we ain't going to let out a peep. Carlotta is a nice girl; Arthur Cushing was the scum of the earth, and . . . Well, I just wanted you to know that we intended to be neighborly and . . ."

"Mr. Burris, you are *badly* mistaken. Carlotta was home early in the evening and . . ."

"You don't have to explain to me, ma'am. I am just trying to tell you that I know how those things are. The newspapers like to get hold of something like this, and once a girl goes through that sort of an experience she's marked for life.

"I know what the facts really are. *I* know that the sound of glass being smashed and the sound of the shot and the woman's scream were long before *you* came over to investigate.

"My wife ain't as close-mouthed as I'd like to have her sometimes, but this is once I've put my foot down and told her to keep quiet about this whole business."

"You . . . You didn't talk to the sheriff and . . ."

"Of course I talked to the sheriff," Burris said. "The sheriff asked me a lot of questions. He asked me if I saw anybody leaving the place and I told him no, that I didn't. And that ain't any lie, because I didn't. Then I told him that I'd first heard the sound of breaking glass and then a shot;

that that was when the killing had been done, I guessed; that it was a while after that when a woman screamed; that I got up a little bit after I heard the sound of the breaking glass and the shot and looked over there and couldn't see a thing. I called my wife, and about that time we heard this woman scream, but neither my wife nor I saw anything *when we got to the window*.

"Now, I didn't tell him that after we'd been standing at the window for quite a while we saw you over there, because I figure that's none of his business."

She said very definitely, "Carlotta was home and in bed long before midnight."

"You don't need to convince me, ma'am. I'm just letting you know that we're trying to be neighborly."

"I know," she said desperately. "You're trying to be neighborly, but in the back of your mind you think that my daughter killed Arthur Cushing."

He raised his eyes to hers. "And you do, too."

The statement was so unexpected, so simple in its complete sincerity, that Belle Adrian found she couldn't meet his eyes.

Sam Burris got to his feet.

"I just thought I'd let you know, Mrs. Adrian. Now, the sheriff is probably going to come to question your daughter. You can tell him that she got home before midnight, and you tell him that I've been here and told you . . ."

"Oh, but I shouldn't tell him that!"

"You've got to tell him that. If you try to act surprised you'll overdo it, just like you did with me when I told you Arthur Cushing was dead. You put on just a little too much of an act. . . . People who live out in the country ain't glib when it comes to talking, but they're sure difficult when it comes to watching. I couldn't tell you just what you did wrong, and I don't think the sheriff could, but you did *something* wrong.

"Our sheriff is plenty cute on things like that. He likes to get people in a corner and try to trap them. Now, you tell the sheriff that I came by here just neighborlylike and told you that Arthur Cushing had been shot."

"At this hour of the morning," she asked. "Certainly he'll wonder why . . ."

"Because," Burris went on doggedly, "I knew that Carlotta had had a dinner date with him last night and I wanted to find out for my own satisfaction just what time she came home.

"I think it would be a good idea if you'd be sort of mad about it—you know, about my getting you up so early in the morning. Up here we're a little different from what folks are in the city. You can tell him I was excited and seemed as though I was just busting with information and had to let it out. I think that's the best way; then you won't have to act surprised or anything, and won't walk into any traps."

He arose abruptly and started for the door. "I guess that covers everything I have to say," he said.

She silently extended her hand.

Burris held her hand for a moment in his callused palm. "You know," he said, "I've always wanted to be what you call a gentleman, the kind that can wrap his tongue around the right sort of words to express any idea. I had to quit school after four years and have had to work hard ever since. . . . We see a lot of you city people up here and we get so we can tell the real from the phonies. Most of them are phonies, but once in a while when we see genuine people we . . . Well, it's sort of an inspiration.

"You and your daughter are like that. I'd like to be able to tell you but I can't."

"I think you've done very well," she said softly.

"I think it would be a good plan for you to get hold of a lawyer. You wouldn't need to let the sheriff know that you'd done it, but . . ."

She said, "Perry Mason, the famous lawyer, is taking a vacation up here. I thought I'd get him and . . ."

"I was sort of halfway thinking of him," Sam Burris admitted. "Of course he comes pretty high."

"I have money," she told him, simply.

"Well," he told her, "I think that'd be a pretty smart thing to do. He's a good lawyer. As a matter of fact, I don't think the sheriff's going to ask too many questions anyway. He knows how people like you folks up here, and . . ."

"I didn't know we were that popular," Mrs. Adrian said.

"Well, you'd be surprised. Us people that have lived up here and farmed the country before it got to be a resort place can tell the regulars from the phonies. You'd just be surprised to find how much talk goes on around about the people who move in here, and how accurate the folks up this way can size 'em up. . . . Good luck to you, Mrs. Adrian, and if there's anything I can do, any help I can give, well, you can count on me."

Sam Burris awkwardly moved toward the door, then paused in the doorway to say, "Your daughter killed him, and she had damn good reason to kill him. Don't ask her too many questions, and don't let the lawyer crowd her too much. There are other girls, and if your lawyer finds them, he can sort of take the heat off of Carlotta. You know what you know and I know what I know. . . . And we both know that daughter of yours is the salt of the earth, a nice young filly that's just as square as they come. Let's give her a break."

And with that, Burris slipped out into the cold, frosty daylight of a gray morning.

When he had gone, Mrs. Adrian stood in the center of the room for a few thoughtful moments, then moved toward the door of Carlotta's bedroom.

"What did he say, Mumsey?"

"Nothing much. He told me that Arthur Cushing was dead."

"How did he know?"

"He heard the shot and the sound of breaking glass."

"He did? When?"

"When it happened. Around two o'clock this morning, I believe."

"Mumsey, did he . . . Did he look out of the window . . . Did he see anyone?"

Mrs. Adrian laughed. "His cabin is three hundred feet from the Cushing cabin, Carlotta."

There was obvious relief on Carlotta's face.

"That's right," she said. "You couldn't recognize anyone at a distance of three hundred feet, could you, Mumsey?"

"Of course not," she said, and then added reassuringly, "Not that it would make any difference. I'm going to go over and see Perry Mason, the lawyer."

Chapter 5

Perry Mason, lying under warm covers in the unheated bedroom of the mountain cabin, noticed that there was enough daylight so he could see the frost of his breath on the cold air.

The cabin belonged to a client and Mason had accepted its loan to get a much needed rest. Now, he found to his annoyance that after four or five hours' sleep he would be wide-awake, his mind racing away at high speed, grappling with the problems of clients he had tried to leave behind.

During the days Perry Mason made it a practice to get so much physical exercise, skiing, hiking, and horseback riding that by nightfall he would be so physically weary he would be glad to crawl in bed by nine o'clock, feeling assured of a long night of blissful slumber. However, by midnight he would snap wide-awake, once more put on robe and slippers, and leave the cold bedroom for the warmth of the comfortable living room, where an oil heater regulated by a thermostat kept the temperature at a constant 73°.

Here the attorney would stretch out in a big chair, pick up a handful of Advance Decisions from the Supreme Court and District Courts of Appeal, and start studying the decisions, carefully noting what judge had written the opinion, at times nodding approvingly, at times frowning or slowly shaking his head as he found himself disagreeing with the conclusions reached by the Court.

Then, once more drowsy, after two or three hours, he would go into the cold, crisp air of the unheated bedroom, snuggle under the covers, drift off to sleep and find to his annoyance that he was wide-awake with the coming of dawn.

The lawyer knew the symptoms only too well. He was so

engrossed in the affairs of his clients that his subconscious mind resented the rest he was trying to take. Della Street, his confidential secretary, had been instructed not to communicate with him except on matters of the gravest importance, and now for four days she had dutifully refrained from even calling him on the telephone.

Today was Sunday and Della was due to arrive sometime in the morning with a brief case full of important matters requiring Mason's personal attention.

Lying there in the cold dawn, watching the mist of his breath drift toward the ceiling and then disperse into nothing, Mason reached a decision. He would return with Della Street that afternoon. It would be better to get back into harness where he could cope with his problems at firsthand. Having trained his mind to work at chain-lightning speed, Mason was now cursed by having developed an elaborate mental mechanism which demanded the stimulus of continued excitement, and which, when deprived of work, could no more slow down than a motor without a flywheel could operate properly.

Mason stretched and yawned, put on his bathrobe, got into slippers, and was headed for the shower when he heard quick, light steps that were almost running, then the noise of feet on the porch and nervous knuckles tapping at the front door.

Frowning, Mason crossed the big living room with its Navajo rugs, reclining chairs, and general atmosphere of rustic charm, opened the front door and looked into Belle Adrian's anxious eyes.

She surveyed the tall lawyer, took in the thick, tousled hair, the granite-hard features, steady, appraising eyes; saw the bathrobe, the slippers and the legs of the pajamas peeping out from under the bathrobe.

"I'm sorry," she said, "so terribly sorry I got you up, but . . . Suddenly I feel awfully presumptuous."

"What is it?" Mason asked.

"I'm Mrs. Belle Adrian," she said. "We are in a way neighbors. I know all about you, Mr. Mason, although you probably have never heard of us. We have the cottage over there on the bay, and I'm in trouble, in terrible trouble."

Mason raised his eyebrows, ran the fingers of his left hand through the thick mass of hair. "What sort of trouble?" he asked.

Mrs. Adrian said frantically, "I know you're terribly high-priced, Mr. Mason, but I'm not a poor woman by any means. I also know you came up here for a rest, that you're badly overworked, that you've tried to keep to yourself and not form any local contacts, that you probably wouldn't consider even taking a case, and yet I . . . I have to talk with you . . . The happiness of my daughter, the . . . Everything depends on it."

"What sort of a case?" Mason asked.

"A murder case."

The lawyer's face softened. *"Now,"* he said, "we're getting somewhere. Come in."

"Oh, I hate to do this, Mr. Mason. I feel so terribly guilty, I . . ."

"Come in, come in," Mason said, cordially. "Do sit down. If you'll just make yourself at home until I take a shower, shave and dress, I'll at least listen to what you have to say and . . ."

"Only I'm so afraid there won't be time for that," she said. "I'm fighting against minutes now. I . . . I ran all the way over here."

Mason indicated a chair. "Sit down," he said. "Want a cigarette?"

She shook her head.

Mason helped himself to a cigarette, saw that she was seated comfortably, and perched himself on the arm of one of the big chairs, drawing his bathrobe about him, inhaling deeply, watching her through the eddying smoke, his eyes sparkling.

"Go on," he said. "Talk."

"I'm a widow, Mr. Mason. I'm living with my daughter, Carlotta. We're up here in the cottage for the season. It's a cottage we own. My daughter is twenty-one. Her father died when she was fifteen. I've tried to be a good mother to her. I . . ."

"You wanted to talk to me about a murder," Mason said abruptly, "and you said the time was short."

"Yes, yes, I know. I do want you to understand about Carlotta. She's a good girl."

Mason dismissed that information with a mere curt nod.

"There's a boy friend in the city who's been very much interested in her. He's a young attorney who's beginning to make his mark. He'd be entirely suitable. . . . I think he's very much in love with her."

"And the murder?" Mason prompted. "Who was killed?"

"Arthur Cushing."

Mason raised his eyebrows. "You mean the son of the banker, the one who's planning to put up the resort hotel?"

"That's the one."

"What happened?"

Mrs. Adrian said, "My daughter has been skiing with Arthur Cushing. There was nothing serious about it. He simply represented masculine companionship. I think, however, that *he* was very attracted to Carlotta, but not . . . not in the way that this other man is."

"In what way?" Mason asked.

She met his eyes and said, "Well—call it a biological urge if you want. Arthur Cushing was that way. There's a lot of gossip around here about him that can't be ignored. He is a professional wolf, using his position, his money, his power to get what he wants. If he can get it he takes it without any scruples, or . . ."

Mason said, "You're looking at the male animal from the standpoint of the mother of a marriageable daughter. Aren't all men more or less . . ."

"No, please, Mr. Mason, understand me. I'm broadminded. I'm not a prude. I understand that the facts of life don't always conform to the theory, but Arthur Cushing was . . . a beast."

"Yet you let Carlotta go with him?"

"Not go with him, Mr. Mason . . . Oh, you're making it terribly difficult for me."

"You're making it difficult for yourself," Mason said.

She said, "You couldn't ever understand this, Mr. Mason, unless you'd been a mother and watched girls grow up. You have to watch over them very carefully during the period in their lives when they reach physical maturity, and then they suddenly blossom into a mental maturity and . . . you don't *dare* to watch over them. If you did you'd break your heart, break theirs, or else force them to show their independence.

"They have to learn certain things for themselves. They have to adjust themselves to life. They have to cease to be children and become young woman, and if at that period of their lives they feel you are watching them, chaperoning them, questioning them, you can't do a bit of good, but you can work incalculable harm.

"It's so easy to ruin irreparably the relationship of mother and daughter. You can destroy every bit of affection. You may leave a certain lip service of respect but you've killed the love."

"All right," Mason said, "you're talking against time. I understand the point you're making."

"You may know about it," she said, "but you can never *understand* unless you've been a mother."

"For the sake of the argument," Mason said, "we'll concede that. You're right, and I can never be a mother. So what happened?"

She said, "Carlotta knew all about Arthur Cushing's reputation. I don't think there's any question that he made passes at her, and," she said, drawing herself up proudly, "he didn't get anywhere, but she liked being on the defensive and he represented a dangerous type of masculine dynamite that she wanted to play with and find out about.

"They were skiing when—well, I think Carlotta would have been very greatly disillusioned if it hadn't been for the accident."

"I heard that Cushing broke his ankle," Mason said.

"That's right, he broke an ankle. It was in a cast. He could get around with crutches and in a wheel chair. . . . He had some colored motion pictures he'd taken on the skiing trip with Carlotta. He asked her to come over and have dinner with him last night and see the pictures."

"What did you say?"

"Mr. Mason, it was the hardest job in my life, but I didn't say a thing, not a word. I tried to act perfectly natural but I knew, of course, what was going to happen."

"What did happen?"

She said, "He was a perfect gentleman until after the dinner had been served and the servant had gone home. Then he became insistent, and then when he got no place he became . . . Well, he lived up to his reputation."

"What happened?"

"I don't know the details, Mr. Mason. I haven't asked Carlotta. Perhaps she'll tell you. I don't want to ask her. I know that she came home, that her clothes were torn, that she was thoroughly angry. She probably slapped him—hard."

"Go on," Mason said.

"Thank heavens Carlotta and I have retained a sane, civilized relationship. She told me what had happened, and we both saw the funny side of it. It was an upsetting experience but we managed to give it a humorous twist, talking about Little Red Riding Hood and the Big, Bad Wolf.

"Then we had a drink and went to bed, but I could see Carlotta was upset and worried, so I went in and slept with her."

Mason's eyes narrowed slightly.

"And so when I heard a woman scream, at around two o'clock in the morning I slid out of bed and tried to locate the direction of the sound. It seemed to have come from Arthur Cushing's cabin and I could see there were lights on over there."

"Carlotta?" Mason asked.

"Carlotta was sleeping peacefully. She'd been nervous and restless right after we went to bed, but when I heard the scream she was dead to the world, so I didn't think it wise to disturb her. I eased back into bed and went to sleep."

"But quite obviously," Mason said, "you didn't sleep long and . . ."

"Do you know Sam Burris?"

Mason shook his head.

"Sam Burris originally owned nearly all of this property on the northwest shore of the lake. He's one of the old-timers here, been farming for years and . . ."

"What does Burris have to do with all this?" Mason asked.

"Mr. Burris was awakened," she said, "by the same noise that I heard—the woman screaming, only in addition to that he heard the breaking of glass, and the sound of a shot. He went over to investigate. He found Arthur Cushing dead in his chair."

"Murdered?" Mason asked.

She nodded. "A revolver bullet in his chest. He notified the sheriff and then he came to tell me."

Mason's eyes narrowed. "At this hour in the morning?"

"Yes. Just as it was getting daylight."

"Why?"

"Don't you see? He knew Carlotta had been having dinner with Arthur Cushing. The servant knew it. The sheriff is investigating the case and at almost any minute now he'll ask Carlotta for her story. And Sam Burris knows what a rotter Author Cushing is—was."

"Well," Mason said, "why not simply let your daughter tell the sheriff what happened?"

"But don't you understand, Mr. Mason, it . . . well, it needs to be tactfully handled. There's a matter of publicity and all of that. If Carlotta's friend in the city reads about it in the papers, and . . ."

Mason shook his head impatiently. "*I* can't keep the thing out of the papers."

"But I thought if we had a lawyer, if we had someone to protect our interests, if . . ."

"As I gather it," Mason said, his voice showing a trace of disappointment, "there's not the faintest possibility that your daughter could be connected in any way with the murder."

"Of course not."

"Therefore," Mason went on, "there's nothing I can do. Your daughter's move is to tell the simple, unvarnished truth. And believe me," he added, looking at Mrs. Adrian meaningly, "any attempt to conceal the truth may have very disastrous results."

"Yes, I understand," she said, refusing to meet his eyes.

Mason studied her thoughtfully. "Look here, are *you* telling me the truth?"

"Yes, yes, of course."

Mason said, "Apparently, Arthur Cushing, disappointed in his attempt at an easy conquest with your daughter, telephoned some other woman whom he knew better, or who he thought might be more amiable.

"Your testimony and your daughter's testimony will be that she was at home. The testimony of Sam Burris will fix the time of the crime. You can corroborate him on that point. That's all there is to it."

"Yes, I suppose so, but . . . I don't know that the sheriff here is too skillful. You know, up until a few years ago this was simply a rural farming community and . . ."

"Go on," Mason said. "Get it off your chest. Tell me what the trouble is."

She said, "I thought that perhaps *you* would know how to get at the facts. The thing we must have, the thing we need more than anything else is to find out who that other girl was; the one who screamed, the one who fired the shot."

"The mere fact that a girl screamed doesn't necessarily mean *she's* the one who fired the shot," Mason pointed out.

"No, no, I understand. That's your legal mind. It doesn't *prove* she killed him. Once her identity is uncovered, however, she will, of course, become the logical suspect. The sheriff will start to work on that theory, the newspapers will play *her* up—and well, Carlotta's name would hardly be mentioned."

Mason nodded.

She said, "I know that you understand about these things,

and I thought . . . well, I thought that you could sort of investigate and . . ."

Mason said dubiously, "I'm afraid the sheriff wouldn't appreciate my help in investigating a murder case. After all, I'm an attorney and not a detective. Moreover, I'm usually pitted against the police."

"I'm afraid," she said, "you don't realize the reputation you have built up, Mr. Mason. You're a lawyer *and* a detective."

Mason said, "I hire a detective agency to do my work. Paul Drake of the Drake Detective Agency has worked with me for years. He's very efficient. We could telephone him and get him to rush some men up here, but even if he used a plane it would be a couple of hours before we could possibly get men rounded up and on the job. Then they'd have to . . ."

"But this is Sunday," she said desperately. "Newspapers are more or less marking time. If we had . . . Don't you see, we have all day. If we can only find this other girl by night . . . well, it wouldn't be too late."

"In the meantime," Mason asked, "what story is Carlotta going to tell?"

"The truth."

"That'll help," Mason told her. He hesitated a moment, then moved over to the telephone, said, "Make yourself comfortable, Mrs. Adrian; there are some magazines on the table."

"Thank you. I couldn't read. I'm terribly nervous."

Mason put through a long-distance call, giving Paul Drake's private, unlisted number.

"Your daughter knows you're up here?" he asked, holding the receiver to his ear.

She nodded.

Mason said, "That might not be too good."

"Why not?"

He said, "Suppose the sheriff comes to ask Carlotta what happened last night and where she was when Cushing was shot. She tells him that she was in bed, that you can vouch for it. They ask where you are and she tells them you've gone over to see me. That . . ."

"Of course," she interrupted, "that's the point I was trying to make, that's why I'm in such a hurry. I *must* get back so as to be there when the sheriff comes. I don't want anyone to know I've been here."

"Better get on back then," Mason said. "I think I understand the circumstances. I . . . Just a minute."

He turned to the mouthpiece of the telephone, said, "Hello, Paul. . . . No, I'm still up in the mountains. Supposed to be resting. . . . Paul, I have a job for you. . . . Yes, yes, I know. Della Street is on her way up here. She'll arrive early this morning, but this is an emergency job. . . . Well, it involves a murder.

"Look, Paul, I want you to put a couple of men on a plane. Come yourself if you possibly can. I need some trained investigators up here just as fast as I can get them here. I can't explain any more over the telephone.

"It's a murder case I want you to investigate. . . . No, it isn't that kind of a deal at all. It's simply the fact that there's a sheriff up here who may blunder around. We want the *true* facts brought out. We want to give the authorities some help. . . . No, they haven't asked for any assistance. They probably won't want any. We'll have to be tactful and . . . You get the men up here and I'll explain it. Can you come yourself?"

Mason nodded with satisfaction, said, "Telephone the airport, get a plane warmed up. The weather is fine up here, with perfect visibility. Cold, frosty and clear, and not even a cloud over the mountains. You can fly up here in an hour and you should be able to get your men and be at the airport within half an hour or forty-five minutes. Get going . . . What's that? . . . Oh, to hell with breakfast," Mason said, "get up here. Yes, it's *that* important."

He hung up the telephone, said to Mrs. Adrian, "Well, I guess that's all we can do at the moment. You get on back, Mrs. Adrian, just as . . ."

He suddenly cocked his head to one side, listening, then

moved over to look through the Venetian blinds. "I'm afraid," he said quietly, "I didn't appreciate the urgency of the matter right at the start. I may have taken too much time asking you for explanations."

"What do you mean?"

"The sheriff's car," Mason said, "is pulling up outside and the sheriff and three deputies, looking very grim, are . . ."

He broke off as steps pounded on the porch and authoritative knuckles boomed on the door.

Belle Adrian turned white to the lips.

Chapter 6

The man standing in the doorway was obviously ill at ease, yet there was a certain determination about him which suggested that while he would advance cautiously, he'd never back up an inch.

Behind him, three men grouped themselves in a position which indicated they were there to back up the sheriff, but were definitely subordinating themselves to his initiative.

"You're Mr. Mason," the man said. "Perry Mason, the famous lawyer. I'm Bert Elmore, the sheriff of this county. I don't suppose you know much about me but I've heard a lot about you."

Perry Mason shook hands. "I know you when I see you, Sheriff, and I'm very glad to meet you. Was there something I could do for you?"

"We'd like to come in," the sheriff said.

"I'm sorry," Mason told him, "I'm busy at the moment."

"Well," the sheriff said, "I think the thing you're busy on is the thing I want to see you about."

Mason raised his eyebrows.

"Mrs. Adrian is in there, isn't she?"

Mason nodded.

"We want to ask her a few questions."

Mason said, "Mrs. Adrian and I were conferring and I would like to finish the conference before we're interrupted. However," he went on suavely, as he saw the dogged expression settle on the sheriff's face, "I'd be only too glad to have you come in and ask questions, subject, of course, to the general understanding, Sheriff, that it *may* be necessary for me to finish my conference with my client during the course of your questioning. Come right in. . . . And these gentlemen?"

"These are my deputies," the sheriff said.

"Come on in," Mason invited cordially. "I think you folks can find chairs."

The four men trooped into the house.

The sheriff, a heavy-set individual in the middle fifties, swept off his huge black sombrero, said, "Good morning, Mrs. Adrian."

"Good morning, Sheriff."

He drew up a chair and sat down. The three deputies ranged themselves along the far wall of the room.

"Won't you gentlemen sit down?" Mason invited.

"This is all right," one of the men said, obviously uncomfortable. "We'd just as soon stand up."

The sheriff paid no attention to them but kept his eyes on Mrs. Adrian.

"I've got to ask you a few questions, Mrs. Adrian, and I hate to do it. I think you know that."

She nodded, tight-lipped.

"Now we went down to your house," the sheriff said, "and talked with Miss Carlotta, your daughter. She said Sam Burris had been down and told you about what had happened last night."

Again Mrs. Adrian nodded.

"He hadn't ought to have done that," the sheriff said.

"Why not?" she asked.

"We wanted to . . . Well, we wanted to talk with you first."

"Why on earth shouldn't Sam Burris do the neighborly thing and tell me what had happened?"

"Well, it's done now. We won't argue about it. I wanted to ask you about Miss Carlotta."

"Certainly."

"She told us," the sheriff said, "that you were over here. She didn't seem to want to tell us about it at first. Was there any reason you didn't want us to know you were here?"

"Certainly not."

"She acted kinda funny."

Mrs. Adrian smiled. "Doubtless due to the fact that Carlotta found herself in a very strange and embarrassing position. She had dinner last night with Arthur Cushing, you know."

"I know all about it," the sheriff said. "We've looked it up. She had dinner over there and the servant got the dishes washed and went home a little after ten o'clock. Arthur Cushing and your daughter were looking at motion pictures in the living room when the servant left."

Again Mrs. Adrian nodded.

"Now, what time did your daughter get home?"

"I . . . I don't know exactly. Somewhere around eleven."

The sheriff nodded slowly. His eyes, gray and thoughtful, studied her carefully.

"What time," Mason asked, "did the murder take place, Sheriff?"

The sheriff ignored the question. He kept his eyes on Mrs. Adrian.

"Did your daughter go out again after she walked home from the stalled auto?"

"No, of course not."

"You didn't go out?"

"I came over here."

"That's the only time you left the house?"

"Yes, of course."

"*You* didn't go to Cushing's cabin?"

"Certainly not."

"Nor your daughter?"

"Of course she did. She went there for dinner, and . . ."

"I'm referring to a return to the Cushing cabin after she had returned to your home."

"No, she didn't go back."

"You know that?"

"Yes, of course. I was in bed with her—and I'm a light sleeper. Why on earth would she have wanted to go back?"

"I don't know. I'm asking you."

"And I've answered you."

"Now, when your daughter was up there," the sheriff said, "she had some rather serious trouble with Mr. Cushing."

"It depends on what you mean. My daughter is a nice girl. Arthur Cushing was not noted for his restraint in certain matters."

"What I'm trying to get at," the sheriff said, "is whether she threw a mirror at him."

"Threw a mirror at Arthur Cushing?" Mrs. Adrian exclaimed.

"That's right."

"Heavens, no. She simply slapped his face and walked out."

"He wouldn't have thrown a mirror at her?"

"Certainly not. He became offensive, that's all."

"When we got up there and looked the place over," the sheriff said, "we found that someone had evidently thrown a mirror. The mirror apparently hit against a window casement and was broken. The window was broken. There were pieces of glass lying out in the yard, and inside the room on the floor."

Mrs. Adrian said nothing.

"You wouldn't know anything about that?"

"No"

"Not from what Carlotta told you?"

"Certainly not. Carlotta doesn't throw things. Carlotta would be a lady under even the most annoying circumstances. I tell you she slapped his face and went home."

"And had the puncture?"

"That's right," Mrs. Adrian said. "Now I may as well tell you the rest of it."

"Just a minute," Mason interposed smoothly. "I think the sheriff has something he wants to say about that puncture."

"Not right now," the sheriff said. "I'd like to get Mrs. Adrian's complete story."

"I think you're taking rather an unfair advantage," Mason said. "Why don't you tell Mrs. Adrian exactly what it is you're trying to get at?"

"I'm trying to get at the facts," the sheriff said, turning slowly toward Perry Mason.

"Exactly," Mason said, "but it is quite apparent that there are certain facts you have that Mrs. Adrian doesn't have."

"Well, that's all right," the sheriff said. "We're supposed to have. We know things about the killing and Mrs. Adrian naturally wouldn't know anything about *those* facts."

There was a certain smugness in the way he spoke that caused Mason to flash a warning glance at Belle Adrian.

"I have nothing to conceal," she said, partially to the lawyer, partially to the sheriff. "In view of what my daughter told me I was somewhat disturbed. I felt that there were certain complications which entered into the picture."

"In what way?"

"We had been friendly with the Cushings. They are, of course, a very prominent family here. I have found the elder Mr. Cushing to be a very fine gentleman. His son, of course, has the reputation of being something of a rake. I wouldn't have thought anything if he had . . . well, if he had . . . well, if he'd made a pass at Carlotta, but when he tried to force her . . ."

"He did try to force her?"

"Her blouse was torn."

"Go on," the sheriff said.

"I knew that when I saw him next it would be a matter that I couldn't ignore. I didn't know whether I should speak to him about it or whether I should simply cut him dead. I was worried. I was unable to go back to sleep. I finally decided that I would simply be very cool, very distant, and very frigidly polite to him the next time I saw him."

"And when was that?" the sheriff asked.

She raised her eyes in surprise. "Why, I haven't seen him," she said. "The next I knew was when Sam Burris told me . . ."

"You're certain that that's the next you knew?"

“Of course,” she said. “Now just don’t interrupt me, Sheriff. I want to explain one other matter.”

“Go right ahead.”

Mason said, “I think it would be wise for you to . . .”

“No, please, Mr. Mason,” she said. “I know exactly what I’m doing and I think I know what Sheriff Elmore has in mind. I want to set his mind straight on it.

“I did hear something very significant at about two-fifteen in the morning.”

“What did you hear?”

“I thought I heard a woman scream, and the scream seemed to come from the direction of the Cushing cottage.”

“So what did you do?”

“I got up out of bed very quietly so as not to disturb Carlotta. I tiptoed to the window. I could see light in the Cushing cottage. I couldn’t see anyone moving around and I didn’t hear anything else. It was freezing cold, so I went back to bed.”

“Your daughter was with you then?”

“She was there in bed, sleeping, peacefully.”

“Well,” the sheriff said, rubbing his jaw, “all this seems to tie in with things and make a picture, but it’s a picture that doesn’t conform to the facts.”

“Well, then your interpretation of the facts are wrong,” Mrs. Adrian said with calm finality.

“Now,” the sheriff said, “I’m kind of worried about this thing, Mrs Adrian, and I have lots of responsibilities, some of which aren’t at all pleasant. Just why did you think it was necessary to come rushing over here to see a lawyer?”

“I’ll tell you why I came ‘rushing over’ to see a lawyer,” Mrs. Adrian said acidly. “I’ll put my cards frankly on the table. I knew that my daughter had been over at the Cushing cottage for dinner. I knew because of the scream I heard that some other girl had been there. I wanted desperately to see if we couldn’t locate that other girl before my daughter’s name was dragged into it.”

“Well, that’s understandable,” the sheriff admitted, stroking his unshaven jaw.

"So," Mrs. Adrian said, "I came over to Mr. Mason and asked him to employ detectives to help *you* in finding the evidence in the case. *That's* the reason I came here."

"Well, now, that's right nice of you, Mrs. Adrian, and I don't mind telling you I could use help in this case, lots of it."

"Well," she said, not entirely able to keep a certain note of triumph from her voice, "that's the truth, and Mr. Mason can verify it."

Mason said smoothly, "For your information, Sheriff, I have just put through a call to Paul Drake of the Drake Detective Agency. Drake is coming up here himself by airplane, and will put himself at your disposal."

"Well, now, that's fine," the sheriff said, "only I don't think I need Mr. Drake's help quite that way."

"No?" Mason asked.

"No," the sheriff said. "I have a duty to the taxpayers and I have the responsibilities of my office."

"But surely," Mrs. Adrian said, "you don't think you're infallible. You said yourself a moment ago that . . ."

"Now just a minute," the sheriff said. "Don't misunderstand me. I can use lots of help but it would have to be done *my* way. If Mr. Drake wants to come up here and investigate the case I'll be only too glad to have him, and if he finds anything I'd be tickled pink if he'd come and tell me what he's found. But I couldn't appoint this city detective as a deputy of mine and take him into my confidence and tell him all the things I was finding."

"Certainly not," Mason said. "We don't expect that, Sheriff. We'll ask Mr. Drake to try and get the evidence in the case, and as soon as he can locate the identity of this woman he'll turn that information over to you."

The sheriff thought a moment, then glanced up under shaggy eyebrows at Perry Mason. "And turn it over to the newspapers at the same time, I presume?"

"Exactly," Mason said.

"Well, I guess that's all right," the sheriff said, "but I'd like to get it first—and have it for a while."

Mason said nothing.

Sheriff Elmore turned back to Mrs. Adrian. "You know, Mrs. Adrian, you and Carlotta are awful nice people. You're the kind of people we like to have up here."

"Thank you."

"And," the sheriff said, "because of that I don't want you to go and get out on a limb."

"What do you mean?"

"Well," the sheriff said, "it's this way, Mrs. Adrian. I don't know whether you've had much experience outdoors or not in tracking and things of that sort, but when frost begins to form it does certain very definite things.

"For instance, last night, as nearly as we can find out, the frost didn't begin to form until around midnight, and then it formed pretty fast in a thick white blanket of hoar-frost. There was a lot of moisture in the air last night and—well, as I understand it, frost is only frozen dew. Perhaps Mr. Mason knows more about that than I do, but anyway, the frost makes a perfectly white blanket over the surface of things."

"Well?" she asked.

"And," the sheriff said, "after it got daylight we were able to see very plainly the tracks of some woman in the frost, a woman who walked from your house over to the Cushing cottage, and then walked back."

Mrs. Adrian's face showed her sudden consternation.

"And," the sheriff went on, "I'm going to be perfectly frank with you, Mrs. Adrian. We found the automobile with the flat tire just like your daughter said, about two hundred yards from your house on the side of the road where she'd pulled off and left it."

Mrs. Adrian said nothing.

"And," the sheriff continued, "we took the tire off to see what had caused the puncture. We found a piece of glass in the tire."

"So what?" Mrs. Adrian said. "A piece of glass is a piece of glass. I daresay that hundreds of thousands of tires have been punctured by pieces of glass at all times and . . ."

"Just a minute," the sheriff said, fishing in his pocket and pulling out a thick sliver of glass. "You can take a look at this yourself, Mrs. Adrian. It's a thick sliver of glass, more than a quarter of an inch thick and it's got silver on the back. In other words, Mrs. Adrian, it's a piece of the antique mirror that was smashed when somebody threw it over at the Cushing cottage. That mirror shattered on the side of the window. Pieces of the glass from it fell out in the yard and down on the inside of the room. . . . Now that tire couldn't have been punctured with that piece of glass unless the car had left the place *after* the mirror had been smashed.

"Yet you say your daughter was home before midnight. Frost didn't start to form as a heavy blanket until around midnight. There are a set of feminine footprints leading from the stalled car of your daughter *back* to the Cushing cottage, then back to the stalled car, and then to your house.

"If these tracks mean anything, they mean that your daughter walked back to the Cushing cottage after the puncture, and then returned to the car, then walked home.

"Now I'm putting the cards on the table, Mrs. Adrian. I want to know the answers. These are the facts. I'd like to have your explanation. I'm not making any accusations—not yet. I'm just telling you how things look. It's up to you, what you want to do about it."

"I think," Perry Mason interposed, "that since Mrs. Adrian is upset and terribly nervous it might be better to postpone any further conversation. I think she's given you all the help she can, Sheriff."

Sheriff Elmore said, "I want to be fair about it. They're awful nice people. I don't want to get out on the end of a limb unless they know what they're doing. Now, do you mean you're telling her not to answer questions?"

Mason held the sheriff's eyes. "No."

"Well, it sounds that way to me."

"No, I'm not telling her not to answer questions. I'm telling you not to ask any."

The sheriff rubbed his jaw, then slowly grinned. "I guess you didn't get your reputation . . ."

He broke off as he heard running steps on the porch outside, then knuckles beating on the door. A moment later, and before Mason had time to get halfway to the door, it was shoved open from the outside. An excited man held out a revolver. A pencil had been thrust down the barrel and the weapon was being balanced with the weight on the tip of the barrel.

"I found it, Sheriff!" the man exclaimed triumphantly. "I found it and I handled it just the way you said to, so I wouldn't destroy any fingerprints. I put the pencil down the barrel and haven't let it touch a thing.

"It's the revolver all right. A .38 caliber, and I found it right there in the weeds, about thirty feet from the stalled automobile where somebody had thrown it as far as she could when she got out of the car—"

"Just a minute," the sheriff said impatiently. "Take that gun outside. I'll join you in a minute. Hold it so . . ."

"You may just as well join him now, Sheriff," Perry Mason said. "Mrs. Adrian is upset and isn't going to say another word to anyone."

"I think," the sheriff said, "she'd better tell us a little more about . . ."

"I don't," Mason snapped.

"Of course," the sheriff told him, "the law comes first in this thing, Mr. Mason. You're a lawyer; you should know that."

"Certainly I know it," Mason said. "If you want to put her under arrest, go ahead and put her under arrest, and I'll go right along with you and demand that she be taken before the nearest and most accessible magistrate and that bail be fixed—"

"You don't fix bail in a murder."

"Are you accusing her of murder?" Mason asked.

"Not yet. Not unless you force my hand."

Mason met his eyes. "All right. I'm forcing it."

The sheriff thought that over.

The three deputies moved concertedly forward, converging on Mason.

Sheriff Elmore motioned them back. "It's all right, boys," he said. "This new evidence indicates it was the woman who drove the car that did the shooting. I think we'll go back and talk some more with Miss Carlotta."

Mrs. Adrian jumped up and started for the door.

"Just a minute," Mason called. "Come back here, Mrs. Adrian."

"You stay right here," the sheriff ordered.

"You can't make me," she said. "I have a right to go anywhere I . . ."

"I've told you half a dozen times," the sheriff said; "I'm trying to keep you from getting out on the end of a limb. You go rushing over to warn your daughter and it'll be the worst thing you can do. It'll look as though you thought she was guilty and . . . Good heavens, Mrs. Adrian, can't you give me a break? I'm trying to put my cards on the table. If you have any way of explaining these facts I want you to explain them to me and explain them now."

Mason said suavely, "I think you're quite right, Sheriff. I think you've been very fair in the matter, and I'm quite certain Mrs. Adrian can explain everything at the proper time."

"The proper time is right now."

Mason shook his head. "Not while Mrs. Adrian is so upset. She's all but incoherent."

"I hadn't noticed she was so upset," the sheriff said. "However, as far as I'm concerned, I want to talk with Miss Carlotta right now."

He motioned to the deputies and they trooped out of the cabin.

Belle Adrian clenched her hand into a nervous fist, pushed the knuckles against white lips.

Mason waited until the door had closed, then calmly walked over to the telephone, said to Mrs. Adrian, "What's the number of your cottage?"

"Two-four-eight," she said. "My God, Carlotta *did* kill him!"

Mason gave the number to Central and a moment later said, "Is this Carlotta? . . . Well, this is Perry Mason, the lawyer. The sheriff is on his way over there with a gun that was found about thirty feet from your stalled automobile. . . . No, that's right. . . . Now listen, we haven't time to argue about it. Simply tell the sheriff that you refuse to make any statement until you have consulted your attorney; that someone is trying to frame a murder charge on you and that you aren't going to say anything until you can figure out who it is.

"No matter what happens; no matter what inducements they try to hold out to you; no matter what threats they make, don't say another word. . . . I haven't time to argue about it, Carlotta. Your mother's here and I'm conveying her sentiments."

And Mason hung up the telephone.

"Now," he said, turning to Mrs. Adrian, "I want to know *why* you went to the Cushing cottage, and *when* you went there."

She met his eyes and said with calm finality, "I didn't go. I don't know who did. It wasn't Carlotta. There may be footprints in the frost, but more frost has formed over them. They'll never be able to identify those footprints—not in a thousand years."

"They aren't yours?"

"No. They aren't mine, and they aren't Carlotta's. . . . Now, let's get one thing straight, Mr. Mason. If they *should* uncover conclusive evidence pointing to Carlotta, then I'm going to give her an easy way out. Then I'll . . . What is it they say—'take the rap'?"

"That," Mason told her with cold finality, "would get you convicted of first-degree murder, when your daughter, by showing she was defending her honor, could get an acquittal."

"And then be branded all her life," Mrs. Adrian said.

"Sure," Mason said, "but how would she feel if people always pointed to her and said, 'That's the woman whose mother was executed for the murder of . . .' "

"Stop it!" Belle Adrian screamed at him.

"I merely wanted to show you," Mason said, "that there wasn't any 'easy' way out. Believe me, Mrs. Adrian, there isn't."

Chapter 7

Paul Drake, looking weary, hungry, and a little annoyed, stepped out of the taxicab, paid off the driver and climbed the steps to the porch of Mason's cabin.

The lawyer opened the door, said, "Hello, Paul! You sure made good time."

"I didn't even wait to shave," Drake said, "and I'm starved. What do you have to eat in the place, and where's a razor?"

"Where are your men?"

"Uptown, eating breakfast at a restaurant. I told them I'd call them and give them instructions. I dashed out here to see what you wanted."

"That's fine," Mason told him. "There's a razor in the bathroom."

"What's the pitch?"

"Get shaved and I'll tell you. What do you want for breakfast?"

"Lots of everything."

"Eggs?"

"Three."

"Bacon?"

"Half a dozen slices."

"Toast?"

"Four or five slices."

"Coffee?"

"A whole pot."

"Fruit juice?"

"Put it on."

Mason said, "I'll throw breakfast together while you shave."

"Della Street got up here yet?" Drake asked.

"Not yet."

"She's due any minute. She told me she was going to get started late last night, sleep somewhere along the road, and get up here early this morning."

"Good girl. I could use her right now."

"She said you were supposed to be resting, but she was willing to bet you were having fits," Drake observed, grinning.

He plugged in the electric razor and ran it over his face while Mason put on a pot of coffee, broke eggs in a frying pan, placed the bread in an electric toaster, and opened a can of orange juice. The bacon was cooking slowly in the broiler.

The aroma reached Paul Drake as he switched off the razor, doused lots of cold water and soap on his face, then applied shaving lotion.

"Gosh, that feels good," he said.

"How long before your men will be ready to go to work?"

Drake looked at his watch and said, "Give them another ten minutes. . . . The guys have to eat."

Mason said, "I have a particular job I want done and I want it done fast."

"What is it? I'll start my men working."

Mason, basting bacon grease over the eggs, said, "Give them a ring at the restaurant, Paul. Tell them to take pencil and paper and go out and jot down the license numbers of every automobile they can find. Divide the town up into streets and blocks and cover the whole thing. As soon as we finish breakfast you and I will get out and try to help them."

"What's the deal?" Drake asked.

"I'm being called on to work in the dark," Mason told him. "I want information, lots of it, and I want license numbers, lots of license numbers."

"Lots of license numbers?" Drake said, coming over to gulp down the fruit juice. "You'll have thousands of them. Good Lord, this is Sunday. There's skiing. The place will be swarming with people. You'll have more license numbers than you can look up in a month."

"That's what I want."

"What do you want with them if you can't look them up?"

"I want them."

"All right. Tell me about the case. What's it all about?"

Mason gently lifted the eggs out of the frying pan with a pancake turner, deposited them on a warm plate, took bacon from the broiler and spread melted butter over Paul Drake's toast.

"This is something like," Paul Drake said, grinning. "You've no idea how good this is going to taste. You've had breakfast, I suppose, and are about ready for lunch."

"I had breakfast about half an hour ago," Mason said. "I'm mixed up in a murder case and it's the damndest murder case I ever had."

"Give me the dope."

"It's a mother and daughter," Mason said. "Frankly, I think the mother feels that her daughter killed the guy."

"Did she?"

"I don't know," Mason said. "If she did, she's a damn good actress."

"You mean playing innocent?"

"No. She evidently is possessed of the idea that her mother did the killing. That's the act she's putting on."

"What does the evidence show?"

"The evidence," Mason said, "is deadly. Right now the sheriff is trying to get some ballistics expert to come up here and test a revolver he's found. Five loaded chambers, one empty cartridge. Nine hundred and ninety-nine chances out of a thousand, Paul, it's the fatal gun."

"Where was it found?"

"Right by the automobile that was driven by the daughter when she left the scene of the crime."

"They can prove that she was at the scene of the crime?"

"That's right."

"Looks like an open-and-shut case."

"They can prove she was at the scene of the crime," Perry

Mason said, "but they can't prove *when* she was at the scene of the crime."

Drake settled down at the kitchen table, devoted his attention to eating, said after a while, his voice thick because of food in his mouth, "That's the evidence that connects the daughter with the crime?"

"That's part of it."

"Good Lord, don't tell me there's more!"

Mason nodded.

"What about the mother? What connects her with it?"

"Tracks in the frost," Mason said. "Tracks indicate that either she or her daughter left the cottage and went to the scene of the crime, perhaps at the time the crime was being committed."

"What does the daughter say?"

"The mother gives the daughter an alibi. The daughter was asleep at the time and can't give the mother an alibi. That's the story both of them tell."

"If it were a lie don't you think they'd have hatched it up so they could have each given the other an alibi?"

"Probably, if they had realized the importance of having an alibi at the time the murder was committed. Once the mother's statement established that the daughter was safely home, she evidently felt that was all there was to the case."

"And the daughter stayed home?"

"The mother says she did. The daughter says she did."

"Wouldn't that stand up in front of a jury, or aren't they that good-looking?"

"They're that good-looking," Mason said. "Both of them."

"Well, then, what do you have to worry about?"

"Somebody left the cottage at about the time the frost was forming a thick white blanket on the ground, went over to the scene of the crime and either that person or another person came back. What's more, the evidence of a punctured tire indicates that the automobile must have been driven away from the scene of the crime *after* the murder was committed, and someone went back to the cottage, returned to the automobile, then walked to the Adrian house."

Drake refilled his coffee cup, poured in thick cream, dumped in sugar, said, "Looks like they have too many suspects, Perry. . . . Gosh, it was a rough trip coming up here. This makes me feel like a new man. Okay, I'll get my men on the telephone."

The detective took his coffee cup over to the telephone, called the restaurant, and instructed his men to start working on automobile license numbers.

"I don't get that, Perry," he said, hanging up the phone. "How are license numbers going to help?"

"I don't know," Mason said. "I . . ."

"Oh-oh," Drake said. "Here's Della Street."

Perry Mason's big sedan drew to a stop outside the door. Della Street got out, pulled out two well-filled brief cases and ran lightly up the steps. Mason opened the door.

"Hello, Chief," she said. "Bet you're glad to see me, huh? . . . I mean the brief cases."

Mason grinned. "Ordinarily I would have been. As it is, we have other matters to occupy our attention. Come on in."

Della Street tossed the brief cases onto a chair. Mason slipped an arm around her shoulders, patted her and said, "Good girl."

"I smell coffee," she said, "and . . . Good Lord, Paul Drake! What are *you* doing here?"

"One guess," Drake said.

"How in the world did you get here? I talked with you on the telephone last night before I left and you . . ."

"Chartered a plane," Drake said, "flew up without breakfast, shaved after I got here. Keep guessing."

"A case?" Della Street asked.

Drake nodded.

"What kind of a case?" she wanted to know.

"Murder," Mason said.

"Who was murdered?"

"A wolf."

"How come?"

"That," Mason said, "is what's bothering the sheriff and it's what's bothering me."

"What does your client tell you?"

"I apparently will have two clients," Mason said. "One of them is a mother who's protecting her daughter. The other is a daughter who's protecting her mother—at least I hope she is."

"Where are they at the moment?"

"The daughter is being questioned by the authorities. The mother has gone to lend the daughter moral support in refusing to answer questions."

"That serious?"

"It may be."

"How come?"

"They talked too much before they knew what the facts were," Mason said.

"You'd better be careful," Drake told him. "You may be defending a guilty client."

"A lawyer has to take that chance," Mason said. "I don't think they're both guilty. They're trying to protect each other. And right now the sheriff has two perfectly good suspects. He can't make up his mind which to grab. He has enough evidence to make a pretty good circumstantial evidence case against either one."

"Could they both have done it, working in cahoots?" Drake asked.

"They *could* have," Mason said, "but I don't think they did."

"What *do* you think happened?"

Mason said, "You're dealing with circumstantial evidence, Paul. It's the best evidence there is, but it's the evidence that's most susceptible to misinterpretation. . . . Right at the moment we're dealing with the sheriff's interpretation of circumstantial evidence."

"So what do we do?" Della Street asked.

Mason said, "Paul Drake finishes his coffee. You have a cup of coffee if you want. Then we take pencil and paper and go out and start writing down the license numbers of every automobile we can find anywhere in the valley."

"You should see the stream of traffic coming up," she said. "People with skis tied to the cars, people with . . ."

"I know," Mason told her, "but I want the license numbers. All of them."

Chapter 8

Harvey Delano, the young attorney with whom Carlotta Adrian had of late been very friendly, parked his car in front of the Adrian cottage and flung open the door.

A slender, small-boned individual, he didn't care much for skiing but was fond of horseback riding. He had only enough skill to ride the steady-going "dude horses," but he went in for cowboy clothes on his weekends.

Now he was wearing cowboy boots, a wide-brimmed Stetson, and Pendletons with a heavy, hand-tooled, silver-buckled belt.

Carlotta Adrian had the front door open and was waiting for him by the time he was halfway across the lawn.

"Oh, Harv," she exclaimed. "I am so glad to see you. I've been hoping you'd come."

"Hi, Carlotta, I wondered if you'd be free. How about a nice horseback ride?"

"You must have left before daylight," she said.

"I sure did. It's the early bird that catches the worm."

"I'm not sure I like that."

He laughed. "Want to ride? How about breakfast? I'm famished."

"Harv, come in here. We're in terrible trouble."

"In what?"

"Terrible trouble."

"Who is?"

"Mom and me."

He circled her shoulders with his arms, led her along the porch into the house. "What's the trouble?"

"Do you know Arthur Cushing?"

"I know of him," he said, his voice instantly harsh. "As

a matter of fact, I've heard you were playing around with him."

"Skiing, that's all. . . . Harv, he's dead. He was murdered last night."

"What?"

"I don't know how to tell you this, but . . . Well, it looks as though someone from this house might have done it."

"Someone from *this* house? Carlotta, what in the world are you talking about?"

"Mother."

"Do you mean that your mother . . ."

"No, no! I don't mean anything of the sort. I am only trying to tell you what's going on, what has happened."

"Is your mother here now?"

"No, she's uptown."

"All right, let's go in and let's get it fast."

"Look," she said desperately, "I want you to get this straight. I personally don't think Mumsey had a thing in the world to do with it. What I'm trying to tell you is that there's evidence, circumstantial evidence, that makes it look—well, rather bad."

"Has anybody made any charges or anything? Have the officers . . . ?"

"Oh, yes, the officers have been around asking questions and all of that."

"And letting it appear that they suspected your mother of . . . ?"

"Mumsey or me."

"All right, put it on the line. What do you want me to do? How much time have we got?"

She said, "Mother has been to see Mr. Perry Mason."

"You mean *Perry Mason*?"

"Yes, he's up here. He has a cottage where he's staying for a few days. A client of his owns the place and he let Mr. Mason take it."

"And what does Mr. Mason say?"

"Mr. Mason told me to say absolutely nothing to the officers and . . . Well, that's what I did."

Harvey Delano said dubiously, "Perry Mason is a great attorney, a very famous lawyer, but I'm not certain that I approve of that. He's accustomed to defending a different class of client. That would tend to direct suspicion to you more than anything you could do."

"I think that's what Mr. Mason wanted."

"Good heavens, why?"

"Because I think he thinks that my mother shot Arthur and I think he wants to mix the thing up so that the authorities won't know which one of us to arrest and will be afraid they'll get the wrong one if they move too fast."

"That may get a little temporary delay but it's not going to help in the long run."

"I know. . . . Harv, I don't know what to do. If I thought Mother killed him in order to protect me, I'd . . . Well, of course, I couldn't let her stand the rap."

"What are you talking about?"

"Just that. I couldn't let her. I'd take the responsibility myself before I'd let her do that."

"Carlotta, are you crazy?"

"No. If she did it, Harv, she did it for me."

Harvey Delano seated himself in a chair, said, "How long have we got before your mother comes back?"

"I don't know. Perhaps half an hour."

"All right. Give me the low-down," he said. "Whom is Perry Mason representing?"

"Well, so far he's sort of representing both of us."

"That's not too good."

"I know it isn't."

"Did you kill him, Carlotta?"

"Good heavens, no! Harv, do you think I'd kill anybody? I wanted to bad enough, but I just slapped his face and walked out."

"All right. Did your mother kill him?"

"It looks as though . . . I want to be terribly careful what I say, but it looks as though someone from this house . . . Some woman must have done it, but if it was Mother, she did things that I just can't understand, Harvey. She did things that deliberately pointed to my guilt."

"Such as what?"

"I drove home. I had a puncture. I left the car and walked. Someone from this house, some woman, walked over to the Cushing cottage, then walked down to my stalled automobile, tossed a gun in the weeds, walked back to the Cushing cottage and then back here.

"Whoever it was didn't realize that the frost would show up tracks—not plain enough to definitely identify footprints, but plain enough to get us into trouble.

"And we fibbed a little to the officers. Mother was trying to keep me out of it. . . . It's the worst mixed-up mess you can ever imagine.

"At the time, I thought Mumsey wanted to have us fib so as to protect *me*. Now I'm . . . Oh, Harv, I'm terribly afraid she was trying to cover up something terrible that happened!"

"Suppose you begin at the beginning," he said, "and tell me everything that happened, and then tell me what you want me to do."

"I don't want you to *do* anything. I only wanted you to understand. . . . It's going to be an awful mess. I'm going to have my name in the papers. There's going to be a lot of speculation, a lot of innuendoes, a lot of things will be said that . . . Well, I wanted *you* to know, I wanted *you* to understand, and after that I don't care."

"All right, what is there for me to understand?"

She said, "Here's the circumstantial evidence. Last night frost started to form—no one seems to know just when—sometime around midnight. I was over having dinner with Arthur Cushing. After dinner he showed me motion pictures of some of the skiing around here and some pictures he'd taken when he was out with me."

"Then what?"

"Then he made a few passes and I put him in his place, or thought I did, and then a while later he started getting rough, and I slapped his face. He grabbed me and roughed me up a little bit. He even tore my blouse. I slapped him again as hard as I could and got out of there. . . . He had broken his ankle and had his leg in a cast. If it hadn't been for that I don't know what would have happened. He . . . Gosh, Harv, he seemed to have no regard whatever for consequences."

"That's what I hear about him," Harvey Delano said, his eyes narrowing. "He was supposed to have a theory that if he just went ahead and got rough no one was going to make a complaint, and if they did he thought he had political pull enough to cover up."

"Well, of course," she said, "you know how it is. No girl wants to come forward and make charges that are going to get her a lot of publicity. It's a lot better to just keep quiet about it and cross it off the books. . . . I know of quite a few men who operate that way, and I've heard girls tell stories of what has happened. I always felt I could take care of myself, but, good Lord, Harvey, he certainly was strong and he just seemed to go crazy. If it hadn't been for that broken ankle I just don't know whether I could have made it. . . . But I made it. I got in my car and started to drive home."

"And then what?"

"Then I had a puncture and left the car standing by the road and walked the two hundred yards to home."

"What time was it?"

She said, "I've told everyone it was sometime around eleven. Actually I think it was about one o'clock."

"Why did you lie about the time, Carlotta?"

"We had to, Harvey. You don't understand. You will when I tell you the rest of it."

"All right. What's the rest of it?"

"Mother got worried about me along about two o'clock in the morning. She looked in the garage and saw the garage was empty. Now, then, she *says* that about that time she heard a woman scream from over in the vicinity of the Cushing cottage. She thought I was still over there."

"Go on," he said grimly. "What happened?"

"She went over there and found Arthur Cushing dead. She came back in a panic and ran into my room and then, of course, got the surprise of her life when she saw I was safely tucked in bed. So I told her what had happened and then she told me what had happened. . . . What neither one of us realized was the fact that she had left tracks in the frost on the ground which were plainly visible at daylight this morning."

"So the sheriff knew she'd been over there?"

"The sheriff knew someone from this house had been over there and that the trip had been made after the frost had formed.

"Now, here's the awful thing, Harv, the thing you're going to have to know. . . . You remember when you were last up here and we were shooting. You showed me how to hold a gun?"

"Yes, yes. Go on. What is it, Carlotta?"

"You left your gun here so I could practice. . . . Well, I was keeping that gun of yours in the glove compartment of the car."

"Good Lord! Who knew it was there?"

"Mother knew it was there. She saw it when she went to put her gloves away. Harv, she *could* have walked over to the Cushing cottage, and . . . Well, perhaps something happened, and she walked right straight back to my car, got the gun out of the glove compartment, went back and shot him, then came home . . . But no . . . she couldn't have done that. . . . The gun was thrown into the weeds after the killing, and . . ."

Delano's eyes narrowed.

"How about when *you* came home? Was there frost on the ground?"

"Yes. I noticed it was glittering and white, but the point is I came straight home. My tracks prove that. I walked straight home. Aside from the one who came to the car from the Cushing place there are no other tracks . . . that is, no footprints. A few cars drove over the road early this morning, but there were no footprints except those of mine from the car to our house."

"What does your mother say about the tracks?"

"Mother, of course, left the tracks to the cottage. I know that. She has admitted it to me, but not to anyone else. She told me that she went over there after she heard a woman scream."

"Did she tell the authorities that?"

"No. What's more, she hasn't even told Perry Mason. That's where she got in bad, because she didn't realize that her tracks had been left on the frosty ground. But, of course, Harv, you understand that if you come right down to it, the prosecution would have to prove the case beyond a reasonable doubt, and at a showdown it couldn't *prove* they were Mother's tracks."

"They could have been either your mother's or yours."

"Yes, or they *could* have been the tracks of any other woman; or, for that matter, a man wearing cowboy boots—if he had small feet. What was to prevent a woman from driving a car down to the front of the house, then walking over to the cottage and back, getting in the car and driving away?"

He was frowningly thoughtful. "Were there car tracks on the road?"

"Oh, yes, of course. There's been lots of weekend traffic all through the valley. Skiing parties, you know, and there was quite a bit of Saturday-night activity around here, quite a few parties."

"The footprints weren't distinct enough so the officers could prove . . ."

"Not a thing," she interposed.

"Did they take your mother's shoes?"

"They asked to see her shoes, and she told them that she had a great many pairs of shoes and that she didn't care to have her wardrobe pawed over. She refused to let them look around the house without a search warrant."

"Then what did she do with the shoes?"

"She cleaned them carefully, of course, but she was afraid . . . Well, she just wanted to be certain, that's all."

"It sounds to me as though your mother is in a pretty difficult position. She'd have done a lot better to have told the truth and . . ."

"I know, but she was trying to keep *me* out of it."

"Do you *really* believe that?"

"Harvey, I just don't know. Sometimes I think that she was worried about me and went over there and . . . Well, Arthur Cushing was in a villainous temper when I left, I know that."

"How about the gun? Have they proved it's the murder weapon?"

"Not yet, but I think they will."

"When they do," Harvey said, "they're going to have enough evidence to . . ."

He broke off as knuckles boomed an imperative summons on the door.

Carlotta turned a white face toward him.

"See who it is," he said.

Carlotta opened the door and found Sheriff Elmore and his three deputies standing grim and purposeful on the front porch.

"I'm sorry to do this," Sheriff Elmore said, "but I have here a search warrant for these premises. I'm serving a copy on you, Miss Adrian, and . . ."

"This is Harvey Delano, an attorney," she said quickly.

Delano stepped forward. "May I ask what's the object of this, Sheriff?"

"I'm sorry," Sheriff Elmore said. "Circumstantial evidence has made it seem that I should search the house. I have here a search warrant and I'm coming in to search the house. You may inspect the search warrant and see that it's all in proper form, and then I'm going to ask you to step to one side and not touch a thing. Both of you sit down there where we can watch you. We're going to search the house. Is your mother home, Carlotta?"

"No, she isn't."

"All right, boys," Sheriff Elmore said. "Let's go."

"Wait a minute," Delano said. "I haven't checked this search warrant yet."

"I have," the sheriff said grimly. "Sit down there and study it all you want to, but don't touch anything, don't try to conceal anything, and don't move around. Come on, men, we're making a search."

Carlotta glanced at Harvey Delano in dismay.

He shrugged his shoulders.

The deputy who was detailed to watch them, said, "If you two will just sit down over there we'll try not to have any more trouble about this than is absolutely necessary."

The pair sat on the davenport, conversed briefly in whispers as they heard the men trooping around the house, drawers being opened and closed, the mumble of low-voiced conversation. The men moved slowly from room to room.

"I think this is an outrage," Carlotta said.

"A murder's been committed," the deputy explained. "The sheriff's trying to do the best he can. People hold him responsible for getting results, you know."

"Well, personally I . . ."

She broke off as Sheriff Elmore entered the room, a gold compact in his hand.

"Here's a gold compact with a diamond on it," he said, "engraved 'Arthur to Carlotta with love.' Do you know anything about that, Miss Adrian?"

She and Harvey exchanged glances.

"It was a present."

"From whom? Remember we can trace this."

"Arthur gave it to me."

"Arthur Cushing?"

"Yes."

"When did you have it last?"

"Last night, I guess. I must have lost it when . . . when I walked home from the car."

The sheriff said, "We found this compact inside a riding

boot where it had been stuffed far into the toe of the boot and packed in with cotton."

"Why, you're crazy," Carlotta said. "That's my compact. I . . . I . . . I lost it somewhere. I didn't try to hide it."

"Then how did it come to be tucked down in the toe of that riding boot?"

"I don't know. I can't give you any answer to that question."

"Moreover," the sheriff said, "I'm going to put some cards on the table, Miss Adrian. When we examined the Cushing cottage we found some powder that had been spilled on the floor and across the shoe of Arthur Cushing. We also found some peculiar slivers of thin silvered glass which we put together and which formed a round mirror. It looked as if they could have been pieces of the mirror of a compact, so we have been searching for a compact as a clue in connection with this case. . . . Frankly, that's one of the reasons we came to make a search of this cottage. We were looking for a compact with a broken mirror."

He snapped the compact open. "You can see," he said, "that the mirror has been broken. There's face powder in here and it looks very similar in texture and shade to the powder that was found at the scene of the murder."

Carlotta raised her chin and clamped her lips.

"What have you to say?" the sheriff said.

"Nothing," she said.

"Oh, look here," Harvey said. "This thing can be explained. Good heavens, anyone could have . . . Why, Carlotta lost that compact. Somebody could have found it and . . ."

"Sure," the sheriff said sarcastically, "then brought it home and hid it in the toe of a riding boot."

Harvey Delano couldn't think of the answer to that one.

"Do you have anything to say, Miss Adrian?"

"My attorney advised me to make no comment," she said. "I have a very complete explanation for anything and everything that may have happened. I will make it when the right time comes."

"I think the right time *has* come."

She shook her head in tight-lipped silence.

"All right, Bill," the sheriff called.

One of the deputies entered the room carrying a pair of shoes. "Do you recognize these shoes?" he asked.

"Certainly," she said. "They're a pair of mother's shoes."

"Not yours?"

"No."

"Would you mind trying them on?"

"I don't know why you ask that."

"We want to see if they fit."

"I can tell you that they do. Mother and I wear the same size shoes. Occasionally we wear each other's shoes."

"Have you ever worn these shoes?"

"I don't think so."

"These are your mother's shoes?"

"Yes."

"That doesn't mean a thing," Harvey said belligerently. "Lots of people wear the same size shoe. Why, look here, I have small feet. I'll bet even I could crowd my feet into those shoes. . . . Here, let's see them. I'll show you just how absurd it is to . . ."

"You just keep your hands off those shoes," the sheriff said, as Harvey reached out to take them. "They're evidence."

"Bosh," Harvey said. "You're afraid to let me show you what a flimsy piece of evidence they are. You can't use anything like that in court unless you can point to some peculiarity in the tracks themselves, and then show that . . ."

The sheriff nodded to his deputy. "All right, Bill," he said. "Let's go."

He tended Carlotta Adrian a sheet of paper on which he had written in pen and ink:

I, Bert Elmore, the duly elected, qualified and acting sheriff of this county, am taking into my possession one pair of lady's shoes and one diamond-studded gold compact with a broken mirror, the compact engraved "Arthur to Carlotta with love."

"Here is your receipt," he said.

He pushed the receipt into Carlotta's hands and walked out, ignoring the fact that the young lawyer was still talking.

Chapter 9

Perry Mason, Della Street and Paul Drake sat in conference with Carlotta Adrian and Harvey Delano. Delano, oddly incongruous with his pale, untanned skin, cowboy outfit and small feet encased in high-heeled cowboy boots, seemed definitely ill at ease as though there was something he had made up his mind to say, yet hesitated to say it.

"I simply can't believe it," Carlotta said. "To think that they'd arrest Mother . . . and yet . . . of course. . . . Well, that's the way the thing is."

Mason said, "Let's get it straight. Do you think your mother went over to Cushing's cabin last night or this morning?"

"Don't answer that question," Harvey Delano said.

"Oh, for heaven's sake," Mason said impatiently. "Let's for once put some cards on the table."

Delano flushed. "I'm sorry," he said, "Mr. Mason, but as Carlotta's friend, as her attorney, I cannot let her become involved in this thing to the extent of making admissions."

"Who's representing her?" Mason asked. "You or me?"

"You are representing Belle Adrian," Harvey Delano said with dignity. "I feel that I have a direct responsibility so far as Carlotta is concerned. I also feel that as this case develops it may be that a personal conflict of interests will develop."

"What do you mean?" Mason asked. "Do you mean she doesn't want me to represent her?"

"I have every confidence in you, Mr. Mason," Carlotta said hurriedly. "But there's a relationship, a friendship between Harvey and me, a . . ."

"Get it out," Mason said. "What's the situation?"

"All right, if you want it right out in the open," Delano

said. "I am advising Carlotta not to make any statements to you or to anyone about what she may have felt about her mother, what her mother was doing, or about what happened last night or this morning."

"You are trying to tell me that you're taking over on Carlotta's case?"

Delano said, "So far, the police have only arrested Mrs. Adrian. Now then, suppose—just suppose, mind you—that Carlotta should have some information which would make her believe that her mother had fired the fatal shot. Suppose they should subpoena her as a witness."

"All right," Mason said patiently, "so what?"

"I certainly want her to be in a position to . . . to protect herself and to protect her mother."

"All right," Mason said, "let's get one thing settled now. You're going to advise Carlotta, is that right?"

"I believe that I have every right as a matter of friendship and . . ."

"You're going to advise Carlotta, is that right?"

"Yes."

"All right then," Mason said. "Go ahead and advise her."

"What do you mean by that?"

"Advise her where no one can hear what you're saying."

"But you . . ."

"*I'm* not advising her," Mason said. "She's your baby from now on. You've taken her case. I'm representing Belle Adrian. You're representing Carlotta."

Harvey Delano's face flushed with angry color, then he got stiffly to his feet. "Very well, Carlotta," he said. "Come on."

"Good night," Mason called as they started from the room.

"Good night," Carlotta said.

Harvey Delano said nothing.

When the door had banged behind them, Mason turned to Della Street and said, "That simplifies matters."

"Weren't you a little rough on him?" Della asked sympathetically.

"I had to be. Either she's his client or she's mine, and I've been laboring under a handicap that's now removed."

"What's that?" Drake asked.

"I couldn't tell whether Carlotta was covering up for her mother, or if the mother was covering up for Carlotta."

"Well, do you know now?"

"Now," Mason said, grinning, "now, I just don't give a damn. I have *my* client, Delano has his."

Chapter 10

Perry Mason's private office might well have been the political headquarters of a candidate on the night of election. A whole battery of clerks was engaged in tabulation activities, four telephone operators called out numbers, four temporary secretaries jotted down these numbers as fast as they were called out.

Mason had explained his theory an hour earlier. "Bear Valley is a hundred and ninety miles away. The people who live up there have nothing in common with the people here. The Cushings had friends and interests here and business interests in Bear Valley. They had no personal friends in Bear Valley.

"Let's assume Mrs. Adrian is telling the truth when she said she was home when she heard a woman scream at the Cushing cottage, and that Carlotta was also home at that time.

"That woman was someone who was friendly enough to be with Arthur Cushing in his cottage at two-thirty in the morning. In that event she'll be friendly enough to attend the funeral.

"If she owns and drives a car, she was in Bear Valley on Sunday morning, and, in company with hundreds of other people, she'll be attending the funeral this afternoon."

"But you can't look up all those license numbers in time," Drake objected.

"We don't have to, Paul. We merely arrange a list and look for duplications. There shouldn't be many."

Drake thought that over, then suddenly exclaimed, "And you'd thought all this out before eight o'clock on Sunday morning and within half an hour of the time Mrs. Adrian called on you?"

It was Della Street who answered the question. "That's what people pay him for, Paul—to think."

"Well, he sure did it this time!" Drake exclaimed.

Two miles away, in a pretentious funeral home, the coffin containing the mortal remains of Arthur Cushing stood on a flower-banked stand. A minister having concluded his remarks, a hidden choir sang softly. Subdued strains of organ music, the heavy scent of flowers, an atmosphere of deep solemnity and the constrained hush of human beings in the presence of the Great Unknown filled the room.

On the outside, Paul Drake's detectives, hurrying around the parking lots, covered all of the parked cars, compiled lists of license numbers which they rushed to detectives who were holding onto telephones in pay stations, feeding the information over the telephone wires to Mason's office.

Mason, Della Street and Paul Drake, taking the tabulated lists of figures, were hurriedly checking them for duplications according to a system which Mason had devised in advance.

Out at the funeral home the mourners filed past the coffin, looking down at the rigid features of the young man who had, according to the minister's eulogy, "been struck down by the ruthless hand of an assassin in the prime of his life, on the threshold of a useful career to humanity and to the community in which he lived."

Then came the shuffling steps of the white-gloved pallbearers; the casket slid smoothly into the hearse, and the solemn funeral procession started for the mausoleum.

Half a dozen detectives on each side of the street carefully checked and double-checked every license number in the funeral procession, adding those numbers to the collection of license numbers which had been picked up in the parking lot and on the streets around the vicinity of the funeral home.

By the time the procession had reached the cemetery, Mason, Della Street and Paul Drake had four duplications of license numbers. Ten minutes later Drake, working in connection with a friendly police official, had the names and addresses of the people who owned the four cars.

One was a real estate agent living in Bear Valley. One was a young man who had been a very close friend of Arthur Cushing, had accompanied him on many of his skiing trips and had twice been involved in some of Cushing's escapades which had attracted unfavorable publicity. The third was a woman who lived in a suburb some twenty miles away, and the fourth was a Miss Marion Keats, who resided in the city at 2316 Huntless Avenue.

Once more Drake's research bureau got busy, and within a relatively short period of time had information which indicated the woman who lived in the suburban town was forty-seven years old, had been a friend of Arthur Cushing's mother, and had felt that Dexter Cushing had, by neglect and cruelty, brought about the death of his younger wife.

This woman had long been very hostile to Dexter Cushing, but had shown a somewhat maternal affection for Arthur Cushing and had from time to time remonstrated with him concerning his life of indolent dissipation.

The report on Marion Keats showed that she was twenty-four years of age; height, five feet four inches; weight, a hundred and fourteen pounds; eyes, hazel; hair, dark.

Mason nodded. "I'll buy the Marion Keats angle," he said.

"The address is an apartment house," Drake said. "She lives in apartment 314. What do we do?"

"There's only one thing to do, Paul. We'll hit while the iron's hot. She'll be returning from the funeral about now. She'll be emotionally upset. There's just a chance, just a bare chance we might be able to get something out of her."

Drake said, "She may have been the one who screamed; she may have been the one who threw the mirror; she *may* have been the one who pulled the trigger on the fatal gun; but somehow I can't exactly see her admitting any of those things."

"Of course," Mason said musingly, "we're dealing with circumstantial evidence. . . . Circumstantial evidence is the strongest of all evidence, but it's astounding what errors can be made in *interpreting* circumstantial evidence.

"For instance, the prosecution has acted on the theory that some woman had a difference of opinion with Arthur Cushing, that Cushing picked up a heavy antique mirror and hurled it at her. She retaliated by shooting him."

"Well?" Drake asked.

Mason shook his head. "It was very much like Arthur Cushing to force his attentions on some girl and *she* might very well have thrown the mirror at *his* head. I can't agree with the prosecution's theory that he threw the mirror."

"You may have something there," Drake said. "A woman would throw things. A man wouldn't."

"Suppose Marion Keats refuses to discuss the matter with you?" Della Street asked.

"That," Mason said, "will be right down my alley. I'll subpoena her as a witness and use her as a first-class red herring.

"This is one of those cases where you don't ever dare put your client on the stand. If she tells the truth, they'll crucify her by showing that it's contrary to the story she told the investigating officers. If she tries to stick to the story she told the investigating officers they'll show up her pitiful, amateurish prevarications."

"And if she keeps silent?" Drake asked.

"If she keeps silent," Mason said, "it will completely alienate the jury and they'll brand her with the stigma of guilt. Therefore, we search for a red herring, and then we start screaming."

"Want company?" Drake asked.

Mason glanced at his watch. "I can't tell what type of approach I'll use until I see her. The preliminary hearing is set for tomorrow. I've had a blank subpoena issued, Paul. I want you to wait just outside the door of her apartment. I'll signal you by hitting the panel of the door. The minute you hear that, ring the bell, and announce that you're there to serve a subpoena on her. Pretend you don't know me."

"You want me to be waiting there at the door right after you get in?" Drake asked.

"*If* I get in," Mason said.

Della Street said, "Threaten to make a scene. She won't like that, Chief."

"She isn't going to like any part of my visit with her," Mason said grimly.

"Just what do you have on her?" Drake asked.

Mason grinned. "Not a blessed thing, Paul."

"Well, be careful you don't let her get anything on *you*," Della Street warned.

Mason said impatiently, "I'm sorry, Della, but there are times when you don't get anywhere by being careful. This is one of those times."

Chapter 11

"This," Drake said, gloomily surveying the pretentious exterior of the apartment house, "complicates the problem. There'll be a lot of red tape. The operator will insist on ringing Marion Keats to announce that we want to see her. She'll say she's too upset and doesn't want to see anyone."

"That's all right," Mason told him. "We'll find a way of getting to her. Now, remember this subpoena is merely window dressing, Paul. She can't be *forced* to attend outside of the county in which the subpoena is issued without an endorsement on the subpoena by the judge before whom the case is to be tried. There isn't time to get such endorsement. I'm simply running a bluff. We can't press the thing too far. Don't argue with her. Serve the subpoena and get out."

Drake nodded.

The desk clerk looked up as Mason and Drake entered the lobby. His face had frozen in an expression of carefully cultivated supercilious superiority.

"Not high class," Mason said under his breath; "just high rents. A place that had *real* class would kick this guy out before his first payday. He's a synthetic snob and I'll bet ten to one he has an itching palm."

"What approach?" Drake asked under his breath.

Mason said, "Loquacious and monetary." He barged forward.

"Good afternoon," the clerk said, "whom did you wish to see, please, and do you have an appointment?"

Mason said, "We're representing the government."

The man's eyebrows arched slightly. His manner became even more distant. "The income tax department?"

"No," Mason told him, "a department for the distribution of governmental securities."

"Indeed."

Mason opened a billfold, took out a ten-dollar bill and said, "In order to get a more equitable distribution of government securities, we're making a series of gratuitous contributions. This is *your* share."

"What am I supposed to do in return for this?" the man asked, glancing hastily over his shoulder to make sure they were alone.

"Exactly nothing," Mason said, "and if you do *exactly* nothing, there'll be ten dollars more for you when we come down."

"I'm afraid I don't follow you."

"Of course you don't," Mason said. "We don't want you to. We're going to see a tenant who lives on the third floor. We don't wish to be announced. In case we *are* announced, this ten dollars represents your entire share of the redistribution of wealth. In case we're not announced, there'll be ten dollars more when we come down."

The man said apprehensively, "I'll have to announce you; otherwise I'd be fired."

Mason remained significantly silent.

"However," the clerk volunteered hurriedly, "if it will be satisfactory I'll announce you after you've had an opportunity to get to the door. . . . I'll explain that some gentlemen pushed past me and went to the elevator; that I found that the elevator had stopped at the third floor; that I'm notifying the janitor and am notifying all of the tenants on the third floor that . . ."

"That's fine," Mason said, "only don't say we're gentlemen."

"No?" the clerk asked, once more elevating his eyebrows.

"Just 'gentleman,' " Mason said, "the singular, one. Do you understand?"

"Yes," the clerk said.

"For twenty bucks," Mason reminded him, "we should be entitled to more than that."

"Yes, *sir*," the clerk said.

"I'll have to know the party," he added. "I can't *really* call all the tenants on the third floor. That would start a riot."

"We're going to the apartment of Marion Keats. I believe the number is 314."

"That's right—yes."

"Yes, what?"

"Yes, sir."

"That's better," Mason told him.

He led Drake past the desk. To the colored elevator boy he said, "Third floor."

Drake said in a low voice, "Gosh, Perry, I didn't think he'd fall for anything that crude."

"I felt sure he would," Mason said. "He was *too* supercilious, *too* much of a gentleman. Those synthetic snobs are always hypocrites. He loves the glamour of acting a part, but whenever a man substitutes supercilious superiority for courtesy you can always try the direct approach."

The colored elevator boy rolled his eyes toward Mason with quick interest. "You all sound like you're talkin' about somebody *I* know," he said, and then his teeth suddenly flashed in a smile.

"Yes," Mason said, as the elevator came to a stop, "the Governor of the state."

"Yes, suh. I *thought* so, suh."

"You wait behind," Mason advised Drake, and, walking rapidly down the third floor corridor, pressed the button of the door marked "314."

A few seconds later the door opened.

The well-formed, athletic-looking brunette who regarded him speculatively was, Mason judged, highly attractive by any standards, despite a certain look about the eyes and nose which showed she had been crying.

"Yes?" she asked. "Who are *you*?"

There was a calm poise about her that caused Mason to revise his entire plan of campaign.

"I'm Mr. Mason," the lawyer said, smiling, "and I wanted to talk with you about Arthur Cushing."

"It is customary for visitors to be announced, Mr. Mason."

"I know," Mason said, making his smile even more friendly, "but under the circumstances it seemed much kinder this way."

"Kinder?" she asked.

"I think you'll understand when I explain," he told her, moving forward with complete assurance.

She didn't step back to let him in. Her own calm matched the lawyer's assurance as she blocked the doorway. "Just *what* did you wish to know about Mr. Cushing, Mr. Mason?"

Mason said, significantly, "Do you wish me to discuss the matter in the hallway?"

"Certainly," she told him.

The telephone began ringing. She frowned for a moment at the interruption, and then said, "Wait here, please, Mr. Mason," and turned toward the telephone.

As she picked up the receiver, Mason calmly entered the apartment and kicked the door shut behind him.

She frowned angrily, then said into the telephone, "Well, you're supposed to prevent situations of that sort. The *gentleman* you mention has just called on me at my apartment and has entered against my wishes. Please see that the janitor comes up immediately, and if that isn't sufficient, I would suggest you call an officer."

She slammed up the telephone, said angrily, "I asked you to wait in the hall, Mr. Mason."

Mason said, "I'm sorry, but I'm quite certain you don't know what I intend to ask you. You wouldn't want me to stand in the hallway and ask that."

Her face was dark with anger.

Mason said, "You were at Mr. Cushing's funeral."

"Certainly. He was my friend."

"And," Mason went on, "you were at Bear Valley the night Mr. Cushing met his death."

She regarded him thoughtfully. "Is that a question?"

"That," Mason said, "is an assertion."

"And is it intended to have significance?"

"Does it have significance?"

"I would say not. I like to ski."

"You were quite friendly with Arthur Cushing?"

"I would hardly have attended the funeral if I had been a stranger."

"Just how well did you know him?"

"What is your occupation, Mr. Mason?"

"I'm an attorney."

"And whom do you represent?"

"At the present time I am representing Mrs. Belle Adrian."

"Mrs. Adrian has been charged with Arthur's murder."

"That is correct."

"I'm afraid that I have nothing to say to you, Mr. Mason."

"Do you, then," Mason asked, "have anything to conceal?"

"Certainly not."

"Naturally you can see that I'm interested in finding out something about Arthur Cushing's background."

"Naturally I can see you're interested in securing the acquittal of your client. If I had any information which would be of the slightest value, Mr. Mason, I would take it to the district attorney. I hope your client is convicted."

"You live here alone?" Mason asked.

"Really, Mr. Mason, you heard what I said over the telephone. The janitor will be here within a few moments."

Mason arose and bowed, "Very well. I'd hoped you would be more co-operative. I thought that it would be better to have you talk to me than to be called to the witness stand to tell your story."

"The witness stand!" she exclaimed scornfully. "What story could *I* tell on the witness stand?"

Mason said, moving toward the door, "I'm sorry I disturbed you. The preliminary hearing is tomorrow. I take it it will be convenient for you to attend?"

"It definitely will *not* be convenient, and I don't intend to be there."

Mason turned and struck his elbow sharply against the door.

"How long have you known Mr. Cushing?"

"As I told you, Mr. Mason, if I had any information that would be of value, I would take it to the district attorney and . . ."

The buzzer made sharp sounds.

"That," she announced triumphantly, "will be the janitor. I think this will abruptly terminate your unwelcome visit, Mr. Mason."

She flung the door open.

Paul Drake shoved a document into her hand, spread out a folded paper and said, "This is an original subpoena in the case of People versus Belle Adrian, preliminary hearing, murder charge. You're ordered to appear tomorrow at ten o'clock A.M. That's your copy."

Marion Keats fell back in dismay, then suddenly, in a panic, tried to push the folded copy back into Drake's hands. Drake merely thrust the original back in his pocket and turned away.

"You'd better come in, Mr. Process Server," Mason said formally. "I want to find out whether this party intends to obey the subpoena."

"This is an outrage," she said. "You can't do this to me. I know nothing that would be of any value."

Mason said, "Your attitude hasn't been co-operative. Now, I'm going to be perfectly frank with you. You don't have to obey that subpoena if you don't want to."

"I don't?" she asked, relief creeping into her voice despite her attempt to control it.

"That's right," Mason said. "That subpoena is not one which will force you to attend a court outside of this county. It has to have an endorsement by the judge after a showing that your presence is necessary, to make such a subpoena valid."

"Thank you for telling me," she said, studying the lawyer

with speculative eyes as she attempted to fathom his reasons for conveying the information.

"But," Mason went on suavely, "unless you endorse in writing on the original subpoena that you will be in attendance, I will now have to go before the judge and make a statement that you are a necessary witness."

"Necessary witness to what?" she asked.

"That," Mason said, smiling with every evidence of inscrutable assurance, "is something I don't want to tip my hand on until you are safely on the witness stand."

"Mr. Mason, I know nothing whatever about this case; nothing that would do your client any good. I . . ."

"I think you do," Mason said.

"What?" she asked.

"Since you have chosen not to confide in me," Mason told her, "I will ask my questions tomorrow on the witness stand. Now the question is, do you wish to endorse on the subpoena the fact that you accept service and that you will be there?"

"I definitely do not."

"Very well," Mason said. "I'll go before the judge and make the necessary showing. That, of course, will focus attention on you insofar as the newspapers are concerned."

"Mr. Mason, this is an outrage."

"I can appreciate your viewpoint," Mason said, "but you must remember that my client also considers it an outrage."

"Your client!" she said scornfully. "The evidence against her is sufficiently black so that she should be . . . Well, I'm not going to condemn her in advance."

"No," Mason said, "it's inadvisable, particularly in view of the effect your testimony will have."

"What do you mean? I don't know a thing in the world about that case. Good heavens, I . . ."

"You seem to know all about the case against my client."

"I read it in the papers. The evidence of the footprints, the torn blouse, the fragment from the broken mirror in the tire of the automobile, the murder weapon found where it had been tossed in the weeds when that girl got out of the car . . . As far as I'm concerned, Mrs. Adrian, and perhaps her daughter, is guilty of cold-blooded, first-degree murder, and I hope she's convicted and given the extreme penalty. Mr. Cushing was a very lovable, magnetic . . ."

"Yes," Mason said, "go on."

"There's no occasion for me to go on," she said.

"Very well," Mason said to Paul Drake. "Report her refusal, then I'll make a showing she's a material witness and that she refuses to attend."

"Mr. Mason," she said, "you're bluffing. You . . . You saw me at the funeral and you . . . You're bluffing."

Mason said calmly, "If you think I'm bluffing, just refuse to sign that subpoena and read in tomorrow morning's newspaper the showing that I make before Judge Norwood, the judge who is going to try this case."

She said, "Mr. Mason, I will be only too pleased to make an endorsement on that subpoena that I'll be there, and I'll *be* there! I defy you to call me to the witness stand."

"Defy?" Mason asked.

"Exactly," she said. "If I'm called to the witness stand my testimony will absolutely crucify your client. I'll see that it does!"

And with that she walked over to the desk, picked up a desk pen, and said to Paul Drake, "Let me have that subpoena, please. I'll show this smart lawyer something he won't forget in a hurry!"

Chapter 12

As Mason and Paul Drake started across the lobby the clerk was at the switchboard telephone endeavoring to square himself with the irate tenant. So intent was he upon his conversation that he didn't even notice the two men who walked quietly up to the counter.

". . . I'm very sorry, Miss Keats. They walked right past me. I *tried* to stop them, but they paid no attention to me. Before I could get out from behind the desk they were in the elevator. . . . It's the fault of the elevator boy. He shouldn't have taken them up until I gave him a clear signal, but you know how those boys are. Sometimes they get pretty sloppy and pretty careless. I'll see that he is properly reprimanded. . . . Yes, there were two of them. . . . No. I said gentle*men*, not gentle*man*. I'm sorry if you misunderstood me. . . . The janitor at the moment didn't answer the telephone. I'm glad they left. Do you want me to call the police? . . . Very well, I see. . . .

"Well, I'm very, very sorry it happened. I, of course, had no way of knowing to what apartment they were going, but since they had stopped at the third floor I decided to ring the tenants that I knew were in . . . Yes, I had seen you come in a few minutes earlier. . . . Well, thank you very much, Miss Keats. It's nice of you to say so. I'm very sorry that it happened, but I want you to understand that it was through no fault of mine . . . Yes, indeed. Thank you again."

The clerk hung up, sighed with relief, then turned to find Mason and Drake waiting at the counter.

"You two!" he said angrily. "You certainly got me into enough trouble, a whole mess of trouble."

Mason said, "I don't think her feelings are as much hurt

as she tries to let on. Here's the balance of the government securities which we are redistributing."

The clerk took the bill angrily and without thanks.

Mason peeled off a twenty-dollar bill and started twisting it in his fingers.

The clerk, at first sullen, gradually became interested as his fascinated eyes watched Mason's fingers twisting this twenty-dollar bill.

"You got out of that very nicely, didn't you?" the lawyer said.

"I barely saved my neck, if that's what you mean."

"It isn't what I meant, but it'll do," Mason said, still continuing to twist the twenty-dollar bill in his fingers.

"You've made me a lot of trouble," the clerk said. "If she should come down and find you standing here talking . . ."

"You can proceed to berate us," Mason said, "for violating the rules of the house, and it would simply confirm the story you had already told her."

The clerk thought that over. Mason remained silent.

"Well, what is it you want now?" the clerk blurted at length.

Mason said, "We were hoping we'd have an opportunity to distribute some more of these government securities."

"For heaven's sake, cut out the comedy and get down to brass tacks. I don't dare to stand here visiting with you. Somebody might come in and . . . What *is* it you want?"

"You're on duty during the afternoons?"

"Yes, I come on at two o'clock in the afternoon and work straight through until midnight."

"You were on duty last Saturday?"

"Yes."

"Miss Keats is a very striking young woman, very beautiful, very interesting. A great deal of fire and personality."

"Well, what about it?"

"A man in your position," Mason said, "would naturally notice a woman like that."

"What are you insinuating?"

Mason merely turned the twenty-dollar bill over and over in his fingers.

"Well?" the clerk asked.

"I'm quite certain," Mason said, "that you would remember whether she was here Saturday afternoon and at what time she left."

"And then do I get the twenty dollars?"

"And about any phone calls she may have had."

The clerk said angrily, "I'm not the sort of person who can be bribed into giving information."

"Of course not," Mason said soothingly, still folding and twisting the twenty dollars.

There was a long moment of silence during which Mason, without even looking at the clerk, seemed concentrating on watching the twenty-dollar bill as he folded it, unfolded it, then drew it through his fingers, moving always in such a way that the denomination of the bill was quite plainly apparent.

"Well?" Mason asked at length.

The clerk said impatiently, "All right . . . I don't know what it is you're up to, but you're going to have to protect me."

"Oh, certainly," Mason said.

"As you so aptly remarked," the clerk said, "Miss Keats is a very striking woman with a great deal of personality. I naturally . . . Well, after all, I'm not given to snooping, you know, but there are certain things that a person in my position notices. It's necessary to develop powers of observation and a good memory."

"Oh, certainly," Mason said again, with a sidelong glance at Paul Drake.

"On Saturday afternoon," the clerk said, "Miss Keats was very much upset about something. She was in and out half a dozen times and then she remained in her apartment, seemingly waiting for a telephone call. The call came in just before nine-thirty in the evening and within fifteen minutes she had called the garage for her car to be delivered. She dashed down carrying a small overnight bag, jumped in the car and drove off."

"You don't know where she went?"

"Certainly not."

"But," Mason said, still twisting the twenty dollars, "you know where the call came from, whether it was local or long-distance and who was calling."

"I don't listen in on the telephone conversations. That's against the law and I could be arrested if I gave out any information about what was said over the telephone."

"Sure," Mason said, "and you wouldn't want that to happen, would you?"

"Definitely not."

"So," Mason told him, "you'd better tell us about the call. I think in the long run that would be your best protection."

The clerk said desperately, "It was a call from Bear Valley."

"Man or woman?" Mason asked.

"A woman."

"And what was said?"

"I tell you I don't listen."

Mason grinned. "Then how did you know it was a woman calling?"

The clerk half-turned away, hesitated, then swung back. "All right. It was the shortest telephone conversation I ever heard. Long-distance asked for Miss Keats and said it was a call from Bear Valley. I rang her and just waited to see that she came on the line. I *never* listen to telephone conversations but I do stay on the line long enough to make certain that the call is completed, that the connection is clear, and then I immediately . . ."

"Sure, I understand," Mason said. "But this conversation was different."

"No, it wasn't. I simply listened to make certain that the connection was clear, and inadvertently I heard the entire telephone conversation."

"What was it?"

"It consisted of one word," the clerk said. "The operator asked for Miss Keats and said that Bear Valley was calling. I know that the call came from a pay station because when Miss Keats came on the line the operator asked if this was Miss Keats, then said, 'Just a moment, please,' and I heard her say to someone at the other end of the line, 'That will be one dollar and fifteen cents for three minutes.' "

"Then what happened?"

"Then I heard the sound of four quarters, a dime and a nickel being dropped in the box, and Central said, 'There is your party. Go ahead.'

"I want you to understand I was listening just long enough to make certain that the connection was in order, and then I was going to clear the line."

Mason nodded.

The clerk said, "It was the craziest conversation I ever heard. No one said, 'Is this Miss Keats?' or, 'Hello, Marion,' or anything like that. A feminine voice at the other end of the line said, 'Yes,' and hung up."

"Just that one word?"

"Just that one word."

"And what happened at this end of the line?"

"Just as soon as she heard that, Miss Keats hung up. I was completely flabbergasted. I couldn't think that had been the conversation, but I hadn't any more than cleared the line than Miss Keats was impatiently jiggling the receiver. I plugged back in, and she said, 'Please get the garage for me and tell them to bring my car up right away.' "

Mason passed over the twenty dollars.

The clerk grabbed at it.

"Haven't you forgotten something?" Mason asked.

"No, I haven't," the clerk said angrily. "The more I think of it the more I think *you're* the one who should thank *me*!"

Chapter 13

Perry Mason, Paul Drake and Della Street were ensconsed in a large suite of rooms at the Bear Valley Inn, rooms that had been fitted up as a temporary office with desks, portable typewriters, dictating and transcribing machines, and an assistant for Della Street.

Because of Dexter Cushing's banking connections, because of the fact that the famous Perry Mason was to be pitted against the local district attorney, the interest of the community in the coming trial had approached a fever of excitement.

Mason, pacing the floor of the sitting room of the suite, was giving a frowning, last-minute concentration to the problems involved.

"It takes three hours and forty minutes' fast driving to get up here, Paul," he said. "That's our time coming up, and we were sailing right along."

Drake nodded.

"Therefore," Mason said, "if Marion Keats left her apartment some time shortly after nine forty-five in the evening, she would have arrived here somewhere around one-thirty in the morning."

"Burris awakened around two in the morning," Mason went on. "It's now been established that the gun that was found near Carlotta's car was the gun that did the fatal shooting, and that it was owned by Harvey Delano, the young attorney, who's been keeping pretty steady company with Carlotta."

"Delano is in the clear on that, though," Drake said. "There are lots of witnesses who can bear him out. The manager of the local sporting goods store, for one. Delano had been teaching Carlotta how to shoot and he mentioned to her that he'd leave the gun with her and she could do some practicing. He bought a cleaning outfit in the sporting goods store and turned it over to Carlotta with instructions on how to take care of the gun. The sporting goods store is the general hangout for an informal club of breeze shooters, so half the town could tell they knew about it if necessary."

Mason nodded thoughtfully.

"So," Drake went on, "that ties the gun in with Carlotta and her mother. Carlotta says she kept it in the glove compartment of the automobile, but of course that's one more thing that she *could* be trying to pull in order to protect her mother."

There was a period of silence, then Drake asked, "Is Delano going to let Carlotta go on the stand? She's made statements to the sheriff that would tend to clear her mother, but what'll happen if she gets on the witness stand?"

"Delano doesn't dare to let her get on the witness stand," Mason said. "They'd crucify her. She's told stories that just weren't true. That's all there is to it. She knows they weren't true, and so do the officers. She'd flounder all around on the witness stand and wind up crucifying herself."

"Yes," Drake said, "those tracks from the automobile showed that she *didn't* get home before midnight. Those tracks were made after the frost had formed a thick blanket."

"Small, high-heeled shoes," Mason said, almost musingly, "leading from Carlotta's car to her home, turning in her gate, then going up to the porch and leaving behind a trail of incriminating evidence."

"Let's look at it this way," Drake said suddenly, "because it's the way the district attorney is going to look at it. Carlotta didn't come home at eleven o'clock the way she said. She came home about two o'clock in the morning. Her mother was waiting up for her. Carlotta told a story that made the mother's blood boil. She immediately decided to go over and have a showdown with Cushing. She walked over to the cottage. Cushing laughed at her. She was in a fury. She knew that Carlotta had abandoned the car, and she knew there was a gun in the glove compartment. She walked to the car, got the gun, came back, shot Cushing, and came home. . . . That's it, Perry. That's the theory the district attorney is going to go on."

"That's fine," Mason said, "but after she shot Cushing, what did she do with the gun?"

"Tried to throw it away where it wouldn't be found. She intended first to put it in the glove compartment and . . ."

Drake came to a full stop.

"Wait a minute," Drake said dubiously, "she *couldn't* have gone back to the car again without leaving other tracks. It . . . Look here, Perry, the whole thing is impossible unless Carlotta killed him. . . . That's what must have happened. Mrs. Adrian got up and looked in the garage to see if Carlotta was home. The garage was empty. So she dressed and went over to Cushing's cottage. She found him dead. She wondered what happened to her daughter and started walking home along the road the daughter must have taken, and came on the stalled automobile."

"So," Mason said, "in place of going directly back home she retraced her steps back to the Cushing cottage and went home that way?"

"Nevertheless," Drake said, "that's what she *must* have done. There was something she was looking for. Perhaps the compact."

"That theory satisfies you?" Mason asked.

"By gosh, it does, Perry. I think it's the truth. I think it's what must have happened. It's the *only* way you can account for the murder weapon being where it was found, and the peculiar setup in regard to tracks."

"That's fine," Mason told him. "If it satisfies you, it'll probably satisfy the jury."

"But don't you see what you're doing?" Drake said. "You're dumping the whole thing in Carlotta's lap."

"Carlotta," Mason told him, "is not my client. Mrs. Adrian is."

Drake regarded him thoughtfully. "What are you covering up, Perry?"

"There's one other explanation you haven't thought of, Paul."

"What's that?"

"That the gun wasn't in the glove compartment, that Carlotta has said it was, so as to help her mother."

Drake frowned. "Then . . . Then Mrs. Adrian must have had the gun with her when she went over to the Cushing cottage?"

Mason nodded.

"Good Lord," Drake exclaimed. "That's premeditation. She must have intended to kill him when she started over there. Then she must have walked down to Carlotta's car for the sole purpose of throwing the gun out in the brush; then she went back to the Cushing cottage, and then home.

"Gosh, Perry, that accounts for everything; the gun, the tracks, the murder, every blessed thing!"

"That," Mason said, "is what the district attorney is going to think, Paul."

"You don't think so?"

Mason said, "We want two things, Paul. One is the woman who screamed. The other is the person who wore the high-heeled shoes that left tracks from Carlotta's automobile to the Cushing house and back—or from the Cushing house to Carlotta's automobile and back."

Chapter 14

The entire community of Bear Valley had turned out to attend the preliminary hearing.

Judge Raymond Norwood, not insensible to the fact that metropolitan newspapers were represented, endeavored to preserve an air of judicial dignity in keeping with the importance of the occasion.

Dexter C. Cushing had employed C. Creston Ives to act as special prosecutor, and if District Attorney Darwin Hale felt any resentment at having to share the credit with some high-priced corporation lawyer from the city, the power of Dexter Cushing's wealth was such that the prosecutor gave no outward sign of such resentment.

It speedily became apparent that C. Creston Ives, despite the wide reputation he had built for himself, was not primarily a trial lawyer, but rather one who specialized in matters of tax, corporation work, and consulations. However, the dignity of his position, his wealth, and professional standing gave Darwin Hale a certain moral support.

The main purpose of retaining the special prosecutor was achieved by his employment. By that very act Dexter Cushing assured the community that he felt Belle Adrian was guilty and that all of his influence and wealth were to be thrown into the battle on behalf of the prosecution.

Darwin Hale, already having achieved a large measure of political triumph locally, was out for the kill, determined to win a case in which the famous Perry Mason was on the other side.

Hale lunged into the prosecution with his characteristic aggressive vigor, but showing plainly that he intended to make only enough of a case to have the defendant bound over for trial. Mason, who had acquired a reputation for stampeding a preliminary hearing into a main event, was to be snowed under—unless, of course, in a last desperate attempt, he was willing to put the defendant on the stand, a development which would have given the prosecution such keen satisfaction that Hale would have offered almost any bait to bring it about. To have Belle Adrian make a statement under oath would give the prosecution a terrific advantage when the case came to trial before a jury.

Dr. Alexander L. Jeffrey, called as the first witness, stated that he had known Arthur B. Cushing in his lifetime, having treated him for a broken ankle which had been incurred in a skiing accident. He had, on the third of the month, been called to the cabin occupied by Arthur Cushing at approximately four-thirty in the morning. He had found Arthur Cushing quite dead as the result of a bullet wound which had penetrated his chest. The time of death, as best he could ascertain from the examination he made at that time, and later on from a post-mortem examination, was approximately between the hours of 2:00 A.M. and 3:00 A.M. that morning.

He further testified that at the time of performing a post-mortem he had recovered a .38 caliber bullet from the body of the deceased. This bullet had caused instant death, and it had been turned over to a ballistics expert for comparison after being properly identified.

"Cross-examine," Darwin Hale snapped at Mason.

"When had the ankle been broken, Doctor?" Mason asked.

"At a date approximately two weeks before the man's death."

"How was it doing?"

"Nicely."

"The leg was in a plaster cast?"

"Yes, sir, the lower leg."

"The decedent could walk?"

"With crutches, yes."

"Without them?"

"No."

"He could move around in a wheel chair?"

"Oh, yes."

"But couldn't as yet exert strain on the leg?"

"That's right."

"And as to the time of death, Doctor? Could the decedent have died before, let us say, 1:30 A.M.?"

The doctor shook his head, then said deliberately, "I am assuming that food was ingested at approximately nine to nine-fifteen. That assumption is based on the statement of the servant who cooked and served the meal.

"The processes of digestion are rather definite, Mr. Mason. The food in the intestine indicates that death occurred approximately five hours after the last meal."

"So," Mason said breezily, "you don't know anything about the time of death except as you base it upon a hearsay statement?"

"No, sir, that is not correct. I believe the body as I found it had been dead from two hours to three hours."

"But when I first asked, Doctor, you based your conclusion upon the time which had elapsed from the ingestion of food?"

"Well," and the doctor shifted his position, "the temperature of the body, which is one factor in determining the time of death, indicated . . . Well, I would say the man had died about two hours before I made my first examination."

Mason gave that statement thoughtful consideration, then slowly nodded and said, "That is all, Doctor."

Dr. Jeffrey started to leave the stand.

"Just a moment," Prosecutor Hale said, smiling. "Mr. Mason has a reputation for being something of a demon on cross-examination, Doctor, so I think I'd better get the matter of his earlier insinuation disposed of by a question or two on redirect examination."

Hale jerked his head at Mason in order to indicate that he was not to be intimidated by Mason's reputation, and then let his eyes sweep over the tiers of faces in the courtroom, faces which for the most part were exceedingly friendly.

Not only did Darwin Hale know most of these people personally, but as citizens of Bear Valley they were only too willing to become violently partisan in watching a local boy make good.

Darwin Hale's glance at the audience as much as said, "Just watch me, folks, this is going to be good."

"Now, Doctor," Hale said, "as Mr. Mason pointed out, your assumption as to the time of death based on the ingestion of food is predicated on the fact that someone has informed you of the time dinner was served?" .

"Yes, sir."

"But this later statement of yours, which Mr. Mason brought out on cross-examination, that the condition of the body itself indicated that death had occurred approximately two hours before you made your examination, *is not dependent upon anything anyone else has told you. Is it?*"

"Well . . . No."

"I think that is all," Darwin Hale said, smiling at Mason. "I just wanted to be certain you understood the witness, Counselor."

"Oh, that's all right," Mason said affably. "I think I understood him. Does that conclude your redirect examination?"

"That concludes it. That's all, Doctor."

"Just a minute," Mason said. "Since you want to get technical about this, Mr. Hale, and since you have commented on my reputation as a 'demon cross-examiner,' I think I had better ask a question or two on recross-examination."

"Go right ahead," Hale said. "Lead with your chin if you want to."

"Now just a moment, gentlemen," Judge Norwood interrupted. "Let's try to avoid these exchanges between counsel. So far they are what one might term pleasantly sarcastic, but experience has shown me that such a situation can develop into one where there is an acrimonious exchange of repartee which lowers the dignity of the court and fosters ill-feeling between counsel. Let's have no more of it."

"Very well, Your Honor," Mason said. "I would like to ask a few questions of Dr. Jeffrey."

"That is your privilege. Go right ahead," Judge Norwood said.

"Now, Doctor, when you stated that from the condition of the body itself you felt that death had occurred about two hours before you made your first examination, you are relying upon exactly what?"

"Temperature for one thing," Dr. Jeffrey said, once more shifting his position on the witness stand. "The temperature of the body undergoes a certain rate of cooling.

"You will understand, Mr. Mason, that the human body is a marvelously efficient example of air-conditioning. Barring reaction to internal infection in the form of fever, the body maintains an almost constant temperature of ninety-eight point six degrees Fahrenheit during life. After death the body cools at an average rate that will give to the skilled medical examiner a very good approximation as to the time of death."

"Quite right," Mason said. "Thank you very much for your exposition, Doctor."

Dr. Jeffrey nodded.

"And, as I understand it," Mason went on smoothly, "you found the body temperature indicated death had occurred approximately two hours before you first saw the body of Arthur Cushing."

"Yes, sir."

"Now, as I understand it," Mason said, "the body temperature decreases at an average rate of one and one-half degrees Fahrenheit for each hour after death. Is that right?"

Dr. Jeffrey put his hand to the back of his head, started moving it up and down along his neck. "Well, something like that," he said. "It is, of course, dependent upon circumstances."

"So I am to assume," Mason said, "that when you first saw the body of Arthur Cushing you determined that the temperature was exactly three degrees below ninety-eight point six, or ninety-five point six?"

"Well, that is not true," Dr. Jeffrey said. "Your assumption is incorrect."

"In what way is it incorrect?"

"Well, I didn't take the temperature the first time I saw the body. It was not until after the body had been removed to a place where I could conveniently do so that I actually took the temperature with a thermometer."

"And how long was that after you saw the body?"

"Approximately an hour, I guess."

"Then I am to assume that the temperature at that time was such as to indicate death had taken place three hours earlier?"

"Well . . . Yes."

"Why do you hesitate, Doctor?"

"I just wanted to be certain I understood the question."

"But you did understand it?"

"Yes."

"And answered it," District Attorney Hale snapped.

"That's right," Mason said. "He understood it and he answered it. And therefore, Doctor, you are now willing to testify that the temperature was ninety-four and one-tenth degrees at the time you actually took the temperature?"

"I didn't say that," Dr. Jeffrey said.

"You said that the temperature indicated death had occurred approximately three hours earlier."

"Yes, sir."

"That was three hours earlier than the time that you actually took the temperature with a thermometer?"

"Yes, sir."

"You have further testified that the average rate change is one and one-half degrees for each hour after death?"

"Well, I so testified in response to a question by you in which you gave that as the rate of change."

"But that is correct, isn't it?"

"Well, it depends."

"What does it depend on?"

"It depends upon the temperature of the surrounding atmosphere."

"Oh, I see," Mason said. "You didn't mention that when I asked the question, Doctor."

"Well, generally, taken as a round average, and within certain limitations, a rate change of one and one-half degrees is a standard."

"Yes, within certain limitations," Mason said, "but as I remember my forensic medicine, Doctor, and I trust you'll correct me if I'm wrong, the limit—the extreme limits of surrounding temperature which justify this rate change formula are between fifty degrees Fahrenheit and ninety degrees Fahrenheit. Anything above or below those temperatures is considered to have a very radical effect upon the temperature change of the body. Isn't that true?"

"That's true," Dr. Jeffrey said, "and I took those factors into consideration."

"What do you mean?"

"The temperature outside was approximately twenty-three degrees Fahrenheit, and since the window had been broken at the time of death, and the temperature of the cabin had rapidly assumed the temperature of the outer air, I took those factors into consideration."

"I see," Mason said. "Now, did you yourself take the temperature of the outer air?"

"No. I secured the records from the weather bureau."

"And how did you know that the window had been broken at the time of death?"

"Well, it stands to reason. It . . ."

"How did you know that it had been broken at the time of death?"

"District Attorney Hale told me so."

"I see," Mason said. "And did he tell you how he knew?"

"He said that a witness, Sam Burris, had heard the fatal shot and the crash of glass, and had gone over to the cabin almost immediately and had discovered that the window had been broken out. He is reported to have found the room in the same condition in which I found it on my arrival."

"So then," Mason said, "when in response to a question by the district attorney, you stated that this estimate that death had taken place two hours before you first saw the body was not dependent upon any statements by anyone else, you were mistaken. Is that right?"

"Well, I thought at the time," Dr. Jeffrey said angrily, "that the question was a little dangerous."

"But you understood it?"

"Yes. I understood it."

"And you answered it?"

"Yes, I answered it."

"And you answered it wrong, didn't you?"

"Well, what else was there for me to do?" Dr. Jeffrey asked. "The district attorney put the words in my mouth, and in a manner of speaking they were correct. They . . ."

"Just a moment," Mason said, as the doctor hesitated. "You don't want us to understand that you would make any statement the district attorney wanted you to?"

"No, I don't mean that."

"I thought you did."

"Well, I didn't. I felt rather uncomfortable about making the answer I did. . . . After all, Mr. Mason, everything in life is dependent upon certain assumptions which are predicated upon information we get from sources that we consider as standard."

"I understand," Mason said suavely. "I didn't think the point was of particular importance, Doctor, until the district attorney made such a point of emphasizing it, so then I thought I would bring out the true facts. Thank you, Doctor, that is all."

Dr. Jeffrey got up from the witness stand as though the chair had suddenly become hot.

District Attorney Hale tried to conceal his embarrassment by making a big show of pawing through papers.

"Any redirect examination?" Mason asked in a voice that was altogether too sweet and conciliatory.

There was a titter from the back of the courtroom.

"*You* run your case, *I'll* run mine!" District Attorney Hale snapped over his shoulder at Perry Mason, still looking through the documents.

Judge Norwood rapped sharply on the desk in front of him. "That will do, gentlemen. The Court will now take a ten-minute recess."

Chapter 15

Mrs. Sam Burris possessed an eagerly inquisitive mind and had an intense interest in personalities. The current topics of the day as discussed in the newspapers were pale and colorless to her beside the intimate bits of daily life involving the citizens in the community.

During the morning ten-minute recess of court, Mrs. Burris, finding herself in a position of considerable importance due to her husband's connection with the trial, couldn't resist the temptation of making a few cryptic remarks to Hazel Perris, the wife of the local butcher.

In response to a statement by Mrs. Perris to the effect that the Adrians were too nice people to really be mixed up in a case of this sort, she said, "Perhaps it's because they *are* nice that they got mixed up in it."

"What do you mean by that, Betsy?"

"Well, after all, Hazel, you know how Arthur Cushing was."

"What does that have to do with it?"

"Well, how would *you* feel if you were having dinner with a man and he wouldn't take 'no' for an answer?"

"I'd pound him on the head with a rolling pin until his ears got to working properly," Hazel Perris said with grim-jawed determination.

Mrs. Burris nodded. "So would I, and that's what Carlotta did, only she didn't have a rolling pin. She used a mirror."

"You're all wrong," Mrs. Perris retorted. "If she'd used a mirror, Arthur Cushing's head would have been bruised and there would have been cuts all over his face and neck."

"Who told you so?"

"Well, it stands to reason."

Mrs. Burris adopted the attitude of a woman who could tell a lot more if she only wished. "You can't always go by what the experts say in a case of this sort."

"Well, that much stands to reason, Betsy Burris, and you know it as well as I do. Besides, didn't your husband say he heard the shot *first* and then the breaking *afterwards*?"

"Sometimes Sam gets things mixed up," she said tartly.

"Is he mixed up on this case?" Mrs. Perris asked with the eager interest of a hound on the scent.

"If you ask me," Mrs. Burris said, "Carlotta slapped his face, threw the mirror at him and walked out. She may have missed him and hit the back of the wheel chair. Then, when Carlotta told her mother what had happened, Belle Adrian just slipped a gun in her pocket and went over there to give Arthur Cushing a piece of her mind. Arthur probably laughed at her, and Mrs. Adrian jerked the gun out of her pocket, probably intending just to throw a good scare into him. It was then that Arthur Cushing picked up that framed picture and threw it at her. When he did that she ducked to one side and that's when the gun went off."

"Bosh and nonsense," Mrs. Perris said. "Carlotta may have been mixed up in the thing to her eyebrows, but her mother doesn't know anything about it. Girls these days are pretty foxy. You can't tell what Carlotta might have been up to—gallivanting around over there until all hours of the night with a man and no chaperone. But Belle Adrian is different. You could never convince me that she would even have gone over to that house at two o'clock in the morning. She's a lady. She'd have waited until morning."

Mrs. Burris started to say something, then caught herself.

"If you knew as much about human nature as I do," Mrs. Perris went on with a certain air of smugness, "you'd know that Belle Adrian isn't the type. . . . I worked as a waitress before I came up here, and I had a chance to study people, and I mean *really* study 'em."

"You and your experience as a waitress!" Mrs. Burris snorted. "Some day I'm going to prove to you that you're wrong. I can't tell you all of it now, but after this case is all over, I'll just make you sit up and take notice. I guess you're not the only one that's had any experience with the public or knows how to judge character. I guess I know a thing or two."

"Betsy, what do you mean? What is it you'll tell me after the case is over?"

"Nothing," Mrs. Burris said. "I was just talking. Now I have to go find Sam for a minute. You'll excuse me."

With sudden, tight-lipped curtness that was entirely different from her usual garrulous self, she turned and walked down the crowded corridor.

For several seconds Mrs. Perris stood looking after the ample figure which waddled down the courtroom corridor. Then, as the butcher's wife turned, she found herself face to face with Sheriff Elmore.

"Well, you're looking thoughtful," he said genially.

Acting on impulse, she took his arm, guided him out of earshot of the other groups in the corridor and said, "Now, you listen to me, Bert Elmore; have you given Sam Burris a good grilling?"

"Sam Burris? Oh, sure. We've got the time element all fixed."

"I'm not talking about the time element. I'm asking you if you've given him a *good* grilling to find out *everything* he knows about the case?"

"I guess so."

She said, "Well, if I were in your shoes, I wouldn't be guessing. And, come to think of it, I guess I wouldn't waste time on Sam Burris, but I would certainly get hold of Betsy Burris and put her through a course of sprouts."

"What do you mean?"

She said, "I mean Betsy Burris knows something about this case she's afraid to tell until after the case is over. She's just as much as told me so, and I think it's something that ties Belle Adrian in with the murder."

"What makes you think so, Hazel?"

"From what she said herself. I'm telling you, Bert Elmore, you get hold of that woman and don't let Sam Burris know a thing about it. You take her in your office and start going to town. I'll bet you'll come up with some information that'll make all the difference in the world in this case."

Sheriff Elmore's eyes narrowed thoughtfully. "Just what *did* she say, Hazel?"

"It wasn't only what she said. It was her manner and the way she acted."

"She said something about some information she could give you after the case was all over?"

"That's right."

"She intimated she and Sam were keeping something back?"

Mrs. Perris nodded.

"Thanks, Hazel," the sheriff said, and, turning abruptly, walked back toward the entrance to the courtroom where District Attorney Hale was in conference with Special Prosecutor Ives.

Chapter 16

At the end of the recess period, when Judge Norwood called the court to order, District Attorney Hale called to the stand a ballistics expert from the metropolitan police force, loaned to the county for the purpose.

This expert witness testified that he had examined the fatal bullet, had checked it with a Colt Police Special .38 caliber revolver number 740818, and that in his opinion the fatal bullet had been fired from that gun. He introduced photographs showing a test bullet fired from the gun as compared with the fatal bullet.

Mason caused a mild sensation by announcing that there was no cross-examination.

The district attorney, in a surprise move, called Harvey Delano to the stand as a prosecution witness.

Delano, slender, well-knit, small-boned, dressed in a well-tailored, double-breasted suit, seemed far more in keeping with his environment than when he had been wearing his cowboy regalia with the high-heeled, hand-tooled riding boots making his small feet seem even smaller, and the big, buckled belt serving to emphasize the man's narrow waist.

"Your Honor," Darwin Hale said, "I have here a hostile witness. He is an attorney retained by the daughter of the defendant."

Abruptly, he swung around to face Delano, said, "I call your attention to a revolver marked People's Exhibit A. I'm going to ask you if you've ever seen that revolver before."

Delano had evidently prepared carefully for his ordeal on the stand. He said, "I am attorney for Carlotta Adrian. As such attorney I refuse to betray any confidences of my client."

"I am not asking you to betray the confidence of your client. I am not asking you for anything you said to your client or anything that your client said to you. I am asking you to testify as to a question of fact. Have you ever seen that revolver before?"

"Yes."

"Whose revolver is it?"

"It is mine."

"When did you last see it?"

Delano moistened his lips with his tongue, glanced somewhat helplessly at the Judge, then said, "I left that weapon with Carlotta Adrian, who is my friend as well as my client."

"So far as you know, was that revolver in her possession on the evening of the second and the morning of the third instant?"

"I have no way of knowing."

"Do you know that it was not in her possession?"

"No."

"When was the last time you had it in your possession?"

"On Sunday of the preceding week."

"That is all," Hale said.

"No cross-examination at this time," Mason said, "but I might care to ask a question later on."

The deputy sheriff who had found the revolver was called as a witness, and told of finding the weapon in "some low brush" exactly thirty-two and one-half feet from the nearest part of the Adrian automobile.

Once more Mason declined to cross-examine.

Dexter C. Cushing, called to the stand, testified that he was the father of the deceased. Quite apparently fighting to control his grief, he testified with tight-lipped determination that the broken frame of the mirror which was exhibited to him by the district attorney was apparently part of an antique mirror which had been in his family for generations, that he had taken the mirror up to the Bear Valley cottage and had told his son to hang it in the living room. The witness had temporarily placed the mirror in the garage.

"Cross-examine," Darwin Hale said.

"Arthur Cushing was your only son?" Mason asked.

"Yes."

"Would have been your sole heir?"

"Yes."

"You are a widower?"

"Yes."

"You are interested in the outcome of this case?"

"Yes."

"You have retained an attorney, the prominent C. Creston Ives, to advise the district attorney in this case?"

"Yes," Dexter Cushing all but shouted.

"For the purpose of bringing about a conviction of this defendant?"

"Yes."

"You are paying Mr. Ives' fee?"

"Yes."

"And naturally you are exceedingly anxious to see the defendant convicted of murder."

"I hope she is convicted of first-degree murder and executed."

"Because," Mason said, "you are anxious to avenge the murder of your son?"

"Yes."

"I take it you do not want to see the murderer of your son go unpunished?"

"I would give every cent I have in the world to see that justice is done."

"If then," Mason said, "this defendant should be innocent, all of the money that you are spending, trying to bring about her conviction, is tantamount to helping the real murderer escape. Had you ever thought about that?"

"Mr. Mason, you attend to *your* business and I'll attend to *mine*!"

"Had you ever thought about it?" Mason asked.

"I have not thought about it, and I don't care to think about it. This defendant is guilty."

"And, upon your assumption that she is guilty, you are exerting every effort to bring about her conviction?"

"You wait until you hear all the evidence," Cushing said grimly.

"Thank you," Mason told him, "I will. I suggest that *you* do, too. Thank you, Mr. Cushing, that's all."

Cushing stalked from the stand.

"Oh, by the way," Mason said as though recalling an afterthought, "this is a question that you can answer from right where you're standing, Mr. Cushing. Did you ever know a Miss Marion Keats?"

"No."

"Ever hear your son speak of her?"

"No."

"Thank you," Mason said, his smile disguising the blow that Cushing's answer had given him, "that's all. Thank you."

"Call Nora Fleming," the district attorney said.

Nora Fleming proved to be a young blonde, well-formed, attractive. She had been employed as a servant by Arthur Cushing, and she apparently testified unwillingly, her big blue eyes downcast, her voice so low that there was some difficulty in understanding her.

Her story came out, a bit at a time.

Arthur Cushing had told her that he was expecting company for dinner on the night of the second. She had prepared a dinner and the "company" had arrived in the person of Carlotta Adrian, one of the defendants in the case. That Carlotta was alone in the car. That the witness served dinner to Cushing and Carlotta Adrian. That the two dined tête-à-tête, Cushing occupying his wheel chair.

District Attorney Hale dramatically produced a torn garment. "Have you ever seen this before?"

"Yes, sir."

"What is it?"

"That is the blouse that Carlotta Adrian was wearing that evening at dinner."

"Please take this blouse and examine it carefully."

"Yes, sir."

"Is there anything different about that blouse now from when you saw her wearing it?"

"Yes, sir."

"What?"

"A jagged tear in the front of the blouse."

"And that was not torn when you saw her there that evening?"

"Definitely not."

"What time did you leave?"

"I would say about ten-fifteen. I had the dishes all done and I asked Mr. Cushing if there was anything else. He said there was not and I told him I would be there at eight-thirty to prepare his breakfast. They were looking at colored movies when I left."

"What time did he usually eat breakfast?"

"Around nine o'clock."

"Cross-examine," Hale said.

Mason regarded her thoughtfully. "Is it Miss Fleming or Mrs. Fleming?"

"Mrs. Fleming."

"You are married?"

"Not now."

"A widow?"

"Divorced."

"Have you lived here long?"

"Two months."

"How long have you known Arthur Cushing?"

"Six months."

"Had you worked for him before you came up here?"

"No. His father hired me after I came up here."

Hale was quite evidently preparing to interpose an objection to any further questions, and Mason surprised the prosecutor by suddenly shifting his line of attack.

"You're familiar with the antique mirror which the senior Cushing had left in the garage?"

"Yes, sir. I have seen it. I have dusted it."

"That was a heavy mirror?"

"Yes, sir."

"How much did it weigh, do you know?"

"No, sir."

"I now show you an antique mirror," Mason said, "which I believe is along the same general lines as the mirror concerning which you have testified, and ask you if you will take this mirror in your hands and tell us whether it is about the same weight and size as the mirror which we have been discussing?"

"What's the object of this?" Darwin Hale asked.

"Just testing her recollection," Mason said.

C. Creston Ives arose, and in the carefully clipped voice of a high-priced corporation lawyer, said, "Your Honor, if any test is to be performed, it must be performed under exactly identical conditions as those which existed at the time of the crime. I do not think Counsel will contend that this mirror is an exact duplicate of the mirror which was in the garage."

"An exact duplicate?" Mason said, in surprise. "Why, certainly *not*! I don't know what gives Counsel the idea that I am performing any test. I'm merely asking the witness if the mirror which was in the garage is of about the same size and weight as this mirror which I am showing her."

The witness, meanwhile, holding the mirror in her lap, lifting it a few inches from time to time so that she could get the weight of it, said, "I think the weight . . ."

"Just a minute," Judge Norwood interrupted. "Did you wish to interpose an objection, Mr. Ives?"

"No, Your Honor, I guess not. I was merely commenting on the law in regard to a test or experiment."

"And Counsel is quite right," Mason said affably. "I am, of course, at the present time only testing the recollection of the witness."

"Go ahead. Answer the question."

"It's about the same size and weight," the witness said.

"Thank you," Mason said. "That is all. The mirror weighs thirty-two pounds."

Judge Norwood said, "It is the hour for the noon adjournment, gentlemen. Court will take a recess until two o'clock this afternoon. The defendant is remanded to the custody of the sheriff."

Mason caught Paul Drake's eye, gestured to him, then, avoiding the crowd, he and Della Street joined the detective and hurried to their suite in the hotel where arrangements had been made for a light lunch to be served promptly at ten minutes past twelve.

As they entered the room, Mason said, "You should have had the dope on that housekeeper, Paul."

Paul Drake said gloomily, "You're not telling me any news. Of course, when we got up here you put us all to work getting license numbers. . . . However, I should have checked her before trial even with all the rush stuff. I'm sorry."

"We've been working against time," Mason said. "Folks told me that the Cushings had a housekeeper who lived up here and had been employed by the elder Cushing, so I hadn't paid too much attention to her. It now appears that Arthur Cushing must have planted her on his father."

"That's what happened all right," Della Street said. "I happened to be where I could watch the father's face while she was testifying. When it was brought out that she had known Arthur Cushing for some time before she came up here, you could see surprise on his face."

"Yes," Mason said, "you can get the picture. Arthur Cushing wanted her to have the job. He wanted his dad to pay the salary. So he had her come up here, and at a propitious moment strike the father for a job, and . . . Well, you can get the entire picture."

"And once the newspaper-reading public gets that picture," Drake said, "it's going to make quite a difference in the case."

Mason frowned. "That's what I don't want to have happen, Paul."

"What do you mean?"

"Let's look at it this way," Mason said, pacing the floor. "Death took place sometime after midnight. The blanket of frost completely isolated that house from all outside contact.

"This young woman had gone home. Carlotta says she'd gone home. The woman says she went home. The evidence on the ground indicates she must have gone home."

"Sure, but she could have returned and shot Cushing."

"Not without leaving tracks," Mason said.

"But look here," Drake pointed out, "a bullet doesn't leave tracks. If she had shot Arthur Cushing through the window from the road the bullet would have sped across the frosty ground without leaving any tracks at all."

"The bullet would have left a hole in the window," Mason said, "and Cushing's wheel chair was turned so that the back of the chair was toward the window. The bullet was in his chest."

"The wheel chair could have been moved afterwards," Drake said.

"The wheel chair wasn't moved afterwards, Paul . . . I'll put it this way. The wheel chair wasn't moved after the window and mirror were broken. I have carefully examined the rubber tires on the wheel chair. At no place can I find where any broken fragments of glass have been ground into those rubber tires. Now, if the wheel chair had been moved after the glass had been smashed, and there was powdered glass around over the floor, some of the glass would have penetrated the rubber tires. And here's one other thing we have to take into consideration, Paul. To have shot Arthur Cushing from the road, required a highly expert revolver shot. The nearest place where a person could have stood on the road and fired through the window is nearly fifty yards."

The waiter brought in lunch and Della Street saw that it was placed properly on the table, signed the check and gave the waiter a two-dollar tip.

Mason said, "There has to be a reason for that mirror having been thrown. That's the real interesting point in the case, Paul. That's where we're going to have to formulate our defense."

"I don't see where it gives you much of an out," Drake said. "The facts show that the mirror *was* thrown."

"*Why* was it thrown, Paul?"

"Well, there are two theories," Drake said. "One is that Arthur Cushing might have thrown the mirror at someone. The other is that someone might have thrown the mirror at Arthur Cushing.

"The district attorney's going to act on the theory that Cushing threw the mirror at an assailant. I have some interesting bits of information for you, Perry. Want 'em now?"

"Shoot the works, Paul. Let's eat."

They sat down at the table.

"First," Drake said, "we checked all telephone calls to Marion Keats' apartment from pay stations here. We found the place but that doesn't help any.

"It's a service station that closes at nine o'clock. It's quite near the Cushing cottage. There's a telephone booth on the outside. The booth remains open twenty-four hours a day.

"Someone put through a call at nine-twenty from that station."

Mason said thoughtfully, "That means someone must have been watching the Cushing cottage, someone who telephoned Marion Keats to let her know that Arthur Cushing was having dinner with Carlotta."

"And, under the circumstances," Drake said, "there's absolutely no chance of ever finding out who it was. The service station was closed, the person slipped into the telephone booth, put through the message, then stepped out into oblivion."

"What else have you got, Paul?"

Drake said, "When the sheriff went over the stalled automobile for fingerprints he found Carlotta's fingerprints, he found her mother's fingerprints, and he found one fresh fingerprint on the door handle that he can't account for. From its position it's probably the fingerprint of a right thumb. My man has managed to get a photostatic copy of it. He'll hand it to me when we go back to court at two o'clock."

"What else?" Mason asked.

"The third thing," Drake said, "probably isn't important. The sheriff has been sweating Mrs. Sam Burris."

Mason frowned. "Now why the devil would he do that?"

"Well," Drake said, "it may be that there's some little discrepancy between her testimony and that of Sam, and the district attorney wants it ironed out before afternoon."

Mason shook his head and said, "He doesn't have to put Mrs. Burris on the stand at all. He can put Sam Burris on the stand and prove what happened, and the wife's testimony would only be cumulative."

"Well," Drake said. "The sheriff has really been working on her."

Mason frowned.

The telephone rang.

Della Street answered, then handed the phone to Paul Drake. "One of your men with a hot tip, Paul," she said.

Drake took the telephone, said, "Okay, let's have it," and sat listening for several seconds; then he said, "Okay, keep 'em under observation as much as you can," and hung up the receiver.

"What's cooking?" Mason asked.

Drake said, "The district attorney's eating lunch in the dining room downstairs. The sheriff telephoned to him a few minutes ago and the district attorney suddenly became jubilant. He went over and reported to C. Creston Ives, and you'd have thought the two of them had just hit a jackpot. They're so tickled they can hardly talk, and they're bolting their lunch so they can dash out to do something before two o'clock. . . . It may have something to do with the angle on Mrs. Burris."

Della Street said, "Mrs. Burris has a reputation for being quite a gossip. She can't keep anything to herself."

"Of course," Mason said, "it *could* be that Sam Burris tried to give Mrs. Adrian a break, and his wife let the cat out of the bag. . . . Paul, when a person applies for a driving license in this state it's usual for the officers to ask to have the right thumbprint. It's placed on the driver's license."

Drake nodded.

Mason said, "Your man has a photostat of that unknown fingerprint, Paul. Get some friendly officer to stop Marion Keats *before* she gets to court this afternoon and ask to see her driver's license. Compare the thumbprint with the license and see if it's her thumbprint. . . . That may be the most important point in the whole case. . . . You'd better telephone him now and have him get started. Tell him to spend money if he has to."

Drake nodded. Holding a sandwich in his hand, he reached for the telephone.

Knuckles tapped on the door in a sustained, nervous knock.

Della Street pushed back her chair. "Who ever *that* is, it's someone in a horrible hurry," she said.

"Perhaps I'll get a chance to finish this sandwich one of these days," Mason remarked, grinning.

Della Street opened the door.

Carlotta Adrian came rushing into the room.

For a moment she was nonplussed as she saw the others in the room, then she regained her composure and walking directly over to the table, stood in front of Perry Mason.

"Mr. Mason," she said, "I can't go through with it, I can't stand it! I've got to get things off my chest. I think it's better for Mother, I think it's better for all of us, for you to know the true facts about what happened and . . ."

"Now, *wait* a minute," Mason said. "You have an attorney."

"Oh, him," Carlotta said. "He's a nice boy but he's only been practicing law a few years. I . . . I think the world of him but . . . Well, this is my own mother . . ."

"Now, all right, let's get this straight," Mason said. "Are you discharging your attorney?"

"Heavens, no!"

"Then I can't talk with you unless he's present."

"But if he were here he'd have fits. He . . ."

"He's here now," Harvey Delano said from the doorway. "What's the trouble, Carlotta?"

She turned to him. "I wanted to tell Mr. Mason something that I think he should know."

"Why didn't you tell it to me, and let me tell Mason?"

"Because I wanted to tell him, and because . . . well, Harv, I felt . . ."

He drew himself up with the dignity of an individual who is still young enough to take himself very seriously.

"You doubt my judgment?" he asked.

"I don't doubt your judgment, Harvey. You're trying to do things for *me*, you're trying to protect *me*, and I think in the back of your mind you feel that my mother shot Arthur Cushing. Now, don't you?"

"That is a matter I see no reason to discuss at the present time, under the present circumstances or in the present company."

"But you do, don't you? You have that idea in the back of your head."

He countered with a question. "Do *you* think your mother shot him?"

"Harvey, I don't know, but I do know that I don't want her being led to the slaughter like a woolly lamb, and there are some things Mr. Mason should know."

"Carlotta, I have told you several times that I didn't want you to talk with *anyone*. I want you to keep absolutely quiet. I don't want you even to tell me certain things about that case.

"It is fortunate that I came here when I did, and heard what I did, otherwise I would have thought that Mr. Mason was guilty of unprofessional conduct in trying to discuss matters with you, and leave me out of the picture."

"I'm glad you understand my position," Mason said.

"I understand it but I don't appreciate it," Harvey Delano blazed at him. "You were remaining within the technical limits of ethical conduct, but that's all you were doing. You could have told Carlotta to have confidence in me and that I knew what I was doing."

Mason said, "I don't know whether you do know what you're doing."

"Are you aware that you're criticizing me in front of my client?"

"You were criticizing me," Mason said. "I merely commented in connection with your statement that I didn't know."

Harvey turned to Carlotta. "Come, Carlotta, you're going with me."

"Harvey, I want to tell you something. I want to tell Mr. Mason something."

"Tell it to me first, Carlotta, and then I'll tell you whether you should communicate the information to Mr. Mason."

"I take it," Mason said to Delano, "your client has not fully confided in you?"

"You handle your *own* business with your *own* client," Delano said, "and I'll handle *my* business with *my* client. I have told Carlotta that I don't want to know anything that she knows until after I know what the sheriff knows. There is, in addition to the professional relationship, Mr. Mason, a personal relationship, and I would appreciate it very much if you would be more considerate of both relationships."

Mason walked over, held the door open and said, "Miss Adrian is twenty-one years of age. She's mature mentally. She can pick her own attorneys and her own friends, and take the sole responsibility in both instances."

Delano whirled to Mason, "Is *that* the best you can do?"

"That," Mason said, "is even stretching a point. Good afternoon."

"Come, Carlotta," Harvey said.

The door closed behind them.

"Well!" Della Street said, and, picking up a menu, made an elaborate gesture of fanning her face.

"That guy sure is young," Paul Drake said. "He's got a chip on his shoulder and a peanut where his brain should be."

Mason, his eyes narrowed thoughtfully, stood by the door, his feet spread wide-apart, his hands thrust into his jacket pockets.

"Well?" Paul Drake asked.

"I wish I knew what it was," Mason said.

"You mean the thing that Carlotta wanted to tell you?" Della Street asked.

"The thing that Harvey Delano *didn't* want her to tell me," Mason said.

Chapter 17

As court reconvened that afternoon there was an atmosphere of triumphant expectancy hovering over the prosecutor's table which immediately made itself manifest to everyone in the courtroom.

Della Street handed Perry Mason a note just as Judge Norwood took his place on the bench. The note said:

> Gosh, Perry, I'm sorry. It isn't her thumbprint. You could have knocked me for a loop.

Mason crumpled the note, pushed it down deep in his side coat pocket, turned to Della Street and whispered, "Okay, Della. Tell him to try the housekeeper. It *could* be her print."

Darwin Hale arose.

"My next witness, Your Honor, will be Sheriff Elmore. I may have to call him again, but I would like to call him at this time to connect up certain matters."

"Very well," the Judge said.

Sheriff Elmore took the stand.

"On Sunday, the third of this month," Hale asked, "did you have occasion to search the cottage occupied and owned by Mrs. Belle Adrian, the defendant in this case?"

"I did. Yes, sir."

"What did you find as a result of that search, Sheriff?"

"I found a broken compact."

"Where did you find it?"

"Wadded down in the toe of a riding boot."

"Do you have that compact here?"

"Yes, sir."

"This is the compact?"

"It is."

"Your Honor, I ask that this be introduced as . . . Now, let's see, the gun was People's Exhibit A, the bullet was People's Exhibit B. This will be People's Exhibit C."

"No objection," Mason said cheerfully.

"What else did you find?"

"I found a pair of shoes."

"Do you have those shoes with you?"

"Yes, sir."

"Was there anything unusual about those shoes?"

"Yes, sir. They had been freshly cleaned."

"What did you find on those shoes?"

"Upon the sole of the right shoe I found a small but distinct stain of blood which had permeated between the sole and the top of the shoe. Inside the soles of both shoes I found small pieces of broken glass which had been ground into the material."

"Could you identify the glass?"

"I was able to do so. Yes, sir."

"How?"

"I used a spectroscopic analysis."

"Do you understand the manipulation and working of a spectrograph for the purpose of making an analysis?"

"No, sir, but I was present when an expert, who is ready to testify, did make that analysis, and I saw the results with my own eyes. Some of the glass in those shoes came from the broken fragments of the antique mirror. The old glass in that mirror was manufactured according to an obsolete formula and contains certain foreign substances which are not present in modern glass."

"I will ask that these shoes be introduced as evidence. The left shoe is D.1, and the right shoe is D.2," the district attorney said, glancing at Perry Mason.

"No objection," Mason said casually. "No objection at all."

"What?" the district attorney exclaimed.

"I said no objection," Mason commented. "We're quite willing to have the shoes in evidence."

Quite apparently this was a distinct surprise to the prosecution. They held a whispered conference, then Hale said, "I have one or two more questions for the sheriff." He turned toward the sheriff. "Have you examined the fragments of window glass from the window of the Cushing cottage, Sheriff?"

"Yes, sir."

"Did you find any fragments with a bullet hole?"

"No, sir."

"Have you examined the wheels of the wheel chair?"

"Yes, sir."

"Find any glass fragments in the tires?"

"No, sir. I may say that from the position of the body and the course of the bullet, it was quite evident that the bullet could not have entered through the window unless the chair had been moved. With that in mind we caused the chair to be lifted very carefully from its position in the room."

Hale nodded approvingly. "Very well done, Sheriff."

"Now, I want you to describe to the Court just what you found when you made an examination of that room," Hale said. "Just describe what you encountered, what the conditions were."

The sheriff said, "There was glass all over the floor. We detected at least five sources of broken glass."

"What were they?"

"A broken mirror, which had been thrown so that apparently it hit the window, shattered and smashed the window. The broken fragments of glass from the heavy mirror and broken glass from the window were all over the floor. Some of the glass both from the window and the mirror had fallen outside and was lying on the ground."

"All right, that's two. What other sources of broken glass did you find?"

"Apparently when the mirror was thrown, or at some time during the melee," the sheriff said, "a big, framed picture had been knocked down from the wall and that glass had smashed. The glass was all lying together on the floor but it was possible to distinguish the individual fragments. The glass from the picture was thinner than that of the window."

"All right, that's three sources of broken glass."

"Then," the sheriff went on, "there was some thin, silvered glass which evidently had come from a small mirror. We managed to segregate all of those pieces and fastened them together on a piece of transparent Scotch tape so that it is possible to see the lines of cleavage and to see both sides of the glass. In that way we have reconstructed the complete mirror."

"You have that with you?"

"Yes, sir."

The sheriff reached in his pocket and took out a small circle of broken glass which had been carefully fastened with Scotch tape.

"You found this in the room with the body?"

"In the room with the body."

District Attorney Hale said, "Now, Your Honor, since we claim this glass came from the compact which has been introduced as Plaintiff's Exhibit C, I ask that it be introduced as Plaintiff's Exhibit C.2."

"No objection," Mason said.

"So ordered," the Court said.

"Your Honor, I am going to ask you to take the compact in your own hands, and then take this mirror, which has been broken and pasted together, and see how perfectly the mirror fits in the compact."

Judge Norwood made the test. Quite evidently he was impressed. He slowly nodded his head.

"Now, then," District Attorney Hale went on, "we have accounted for four sources of broken glass. The windowpane, the antique mirror, the framed picture, the mirror from the compact. What was the fifth source, Sheriff?"

"Well," the sheriff said, "that was rather easy to distinguish. There was a glass, apparently a highball glass, lying shattered into small fragments on the floor."

"What about the distribution of these fragments of glass from the tumbler, Sheriff?"

"Well, it was just sort of kicked all around over the floor. You couldn't figure out what had caused . . ."

"Never mind that, Sheriff. I just want to know the distribution of the glass from the tumbler."

"Well, the tumbler pieces were right around the right side of the wheel chair. The compact mirror was there, also. The rest of the glass was all over the place. There was a pile, of course, by the window. It was pretty thick there, but the chair was some six feet away from the window and there was glass all around the chair. That broken glass had been kicked around as though there had been some sort of a struggle."

The district attorney said, "Your Honor, there is one other piece of evidence I want to introduce. A piece of glass which was found in the tire of the Adrian automobile, but the sheriff doesn't have that with him right at the moment. I ask permission of the Court to put the sheriff on again a little later."

"Very well, that permission is granted."

"Under those circumstances you may cross-examine," Hale said.

"You say the glass had been kicked around as though there had been a struggle?" Mason said.

"That's right. Yes, sir."

"When did the struggle take place? Before the glass was smashed or afterwards?"

The sheriff smiled dryly. "If the glass had been kicked around as the result of a struggle, Mr. Mason, the struggle must have taken place after the glass was smashed."

"Exactly," Mason said, "but while you found glass all around the wheel chair, you didn't find any fragments embedded in the rubber tires?"

"No, sir."

"Those rubber tires were soft enough to have picked up glass?"

"Oh, yes. They were sort of a spongy rubber, very resilient. Not pneumatic tires, but a soft, spongy rubber. They would very readily have picked up glass."

"So when this struggle took place," Mason said, "Arthur Cushing wasn't taking part in it?"

"He may have been dead," the sheriff said dryly.

"Your assumption is then that Arthur Cushing was shot and the struggle took place after his death?"

"Apparently."

"One party to the struggle must have been the murderer?"

"I would assume so, Mr. Mason."

"And who was the other one?"

"That, of course, I can't tell."

"Yet," Mason said, "there are only one set of tracks leaving the house."

"Now, there," the sheriff admitted, "you have me stumped, Mr. Mason. I'm reporting the physical facts. I'm giving you the circumstantial evidence as it exists."

"As I understand it," Mason said, "you examined the tracks very carefully."

"We did. Yes, sir."

"How many sets of tracks did you find?"

"There were the tracks made by Mrs. Adrian—you'll pardon me, Mr. Mason, that's a conclusion. There were the tracks from the Adrian house to the Cushing cottage, and it was possible to see where some person, apparently the one who had made those tracks, had walked up to the front door, then around the house and around the driveway, then to the back part of the house and entered through the back door, then, later on, left through the back door and retraced her steps back to the Adrian cottage.

"Then there was another set of tracks, or what we assume is another set of tracks, leaving the front door of the Cushing cottage, going to the Adrian automobile and back—or vice versa. Then there are tracks leading from the Adrian automobile to the Adrian cottage."

"In other words," Mason said, "a person driving the Adrian automobile, having stopped the car, *could* have got out from behind the steering wheel, walked back to the Cushing cottage, then returned to the automobile, then from the automobile gone to the Adrian cottage. Is that right?"

"Yes, sir."

"Could you tell that those were all the same tracks?"

"They looked the same. They are about the same size. They were made with fairly high-heeled shoes. That's about all you can tell about them. The heels, however, were rather broad, not quite the narrow, pointed heels of a woman's dress shoes, but more the type of sensible walking shoes with a relatively broad heel."

"And the tracks from the Adrian cottage to the Cushing cottage?"

"Those could well have been made with the same shoes or with shoes of approximately the same size and description."

"So," Mason said, "the most you can get out of it is that you have two sets of tracks?"

"That's right."

"Were there any more tracks?"

"Only those made by Sam Burris when he went over to investigate, and my tracks and the tracks of two deputies. . . . And I may state, Mr. Mason, we were particularly careful to see that our tracks did not cross those of the others or obscure them in any way. We were very careful to form in single file, and, as far as possible, one person walked in the footsteps of the other."

"So," Mason said, "the best you can make of it is that if there was a struggle in the cottage, there were only two persons who could have participated in that struggle. One of them is the woman, whoever she was, who made the tracks from the Adrian cottage to the Cushing cottage, and the other one was the person who made tracks from the automobile to the Cushing cottage."

"That's right. Yes, sir."

"Those were the only two people who could have engaged in a struggle after the murder was committed?"

"Yes, sir," the sheriff said, and then added dryly, "And I may point out that both of those tracks terminated at the Adrian cottage—and that Carlotta's blouse was torn."

"Thank you," Mason said. "I think that's all for the moment."

Hale exchanged a quick glance with Ives, then with an air of triumph he was unable to conceal, said, "My next witness will be Mrs. Sam Burris."

Mrs. Sam Burris, a big woman, looking distinctly uncomfortable, waddled her way to the witness stand, was sworn, gave her name and address, then turned tired eyes to the district attorney.

"Directing your attention to the early morning hours of the third of this month," the district attorney said, "did you have occasion to notice the Cushing cottage?"

"I did. Yes, sir."

"What was that occasion?"

"My husband had heard . . ."

"Never mind what your husband had heard. Just what caused you to look over there?"

"My husband wakened me."

"And did he tell you something?"

"Yes."

"Never mind what it was he told you, but what did *you* do after *he* made this statement to you?"

"I got up and looked over at the Cushing cottage."

"What time was it?"

"As nearly as I can tell, it was right around two-thirty in the morning."

"And what did you see?"

"I saw lights in the cottage."

"Did you use any optical aid?"

"Yes. We have a thirty-power telescope."

"And did you use that?"

"Yes, sir."

"What did you see?"

"I saw broken glass. I saw a window which had been broken out, and the broken glass was on the window sill and some of it was on the ground underneath the window where it was reflecting back some of the light from the interior of the room."

"The window was broken?"

"Yes."

"There were no shades drawn?"

"Not on that window, no."

"And did you hear anything?"

"Just before I got up out of bed I heard a woman scream."

"Of your own knowledge, do you *know* who that woman was?"

"No, sir."

"And did you see any individual in that house at that time?"

"Yes, sir, some five or ten minutes after we heard the scream."

"Did you recognize that individual?"

"Yes, sir."

"Who was it?"

"Mrs. Belle Adrian, the defendant sitting here in court."

"You may cross-examine," the district attorney said.

Mason smiled reassuringly at Mrs. Burris.

"The district attorney," Mason said, "was, of course, very conscientious in trying to keep you from giving any hearsay evidence, but as between us it doesn't make any difference. What was it your husband told you which caused you to get up out of bed to look over at the Cushing cottage, Mrs. Burris?"

She said, "He told me that he'd heard something that sounded like breaking glass, and he thought a shot. He said he got up out of bed and looked but couldn't see anything."

"You didn't hear these sounds?"

"No, sir. I'm a heavy sleeper. Sam's a light sleeper."

"But you got up to look?"

"Yes. I wanted to see what was going on."

"Was it a habit of yours?"

"Well, we'd . . . We'd had occasion to look over there sometimes before. The window isn't visible from any cottage except ours. Arthur Cushing very seldom pulled that shade down and . . ."

"And what have you seen on those occasions?" Mason asked.

"Objected to as incompetent, irrelevant and immaterial. Not proper cross-examination," Darwin Hale said.

"Sustained," Judge Norwood said.

"And on this particular occasion you saw Mrs. Belle Adrian, the defendant in this case?"

"Yes, sir."

"Did you see anybody else?"

"No, sir."

"Could you see what she was doing?"

"Well, I saw her stoop over as though to pick up something and I saw her moving around back and forth across the window once or twice."

"You didn't see her lips moving as though she might have been talking to anyone?"

"No, sir."

"Didn't see anyone else?"

"No, sir."

"And then what?"

"Well, I noticed the window was smashed out so I insisted my husband should go over there and see what was wrong. He found . . ."

"Now, you don't know just what he found, do you?"

"Well, he told me what he found."

"I think we'd better let him tell about that," Mason said. "That's all, Mrs. Burris. Thank you very much. I just wanted to get the situation straight."

"That's all your cross-examination?" Ives asked.

"That's all of it," Mason said.

"Very well," the district attorney said, "I'll call Mr. Sam Burris to the stand. Of course, Your Honor, the Court will understand that at this time we're simply trying to give the Court a quick picture of what happened. For the purpose of this hearing it is only necessary for us to show that a crime has been committed and to show that there is reasonable ground for believing the defendant committed that crime. Then the Court makes an order binding the defendant over for trial. The trial, of course, will take place in front of a jury and . . ."

"You don't need to educate the Court on the law," Judge Norwood said. "I think the Court understands the law, Mr. District Attorney. Just go right ahead and put on your case."

"Very well, Your Honor. I wanted you to understand why I'm not showing all of my hand."

"You show enough of your hand to give the Court reason to bind the defendant over," Judge Norwood said, "or the Court won't bind her over."

"Don't worry," the prosecutor said grimly, "I'll do that."

"You seem to be the one who's doing the worrying," Judge Norwood said. "The Court is fully familiar with the law and the Court knows that you know the Court is fully familiar with the law. If you want to make any statements for the benefit of spectators in the courtroom, make them at the proper time and in the proper manner, and to the spectators and not the Court. Now, call your next witness."

"Yes, Your Honor," Hale said, somewhat crestfallen. "Mr. Sam Burris, will you come forward and be sworn, please?"

Sam Burris came to the witness stand looking very much like a wet cat that has been caught out in a thunderstorm and is torn between emotions of anger and humiliation.

District Attorney Hale was coldly merciless. "You had occasion to look at the Cushing cottage on the morning of the second?"

"Yes, sir."

"At what time?"

"Right around two-thirty, about two-twenty-five, I guess."

"What caused you to look at the cottage at that hour?"

"I am a very light sleeper. I was lying in bed and was a little restless. I heard the crash of glass and the sound of a shot, and wondered about it. Then I started to drift off back to sleep again, but I kept worrying. I looked out but didn't see anything. I spoke to my wife, wakened her, and then we heard a woman scream. So I got up again and we both looked out of the window."

"What did you see?"

"I saw lights on in the Cushing cottage and I told my wife . . ."

"Never mind what you told your wife. What did you do?"

"I looked at the Cushing cottage. My wife looked at the Cushing cottage."

"Did you use any optical aid?"

"A thirty-power telescope."

"What did you see?"

"I saw the broken window, the mirror that was smashed, and then I saw Mrs. Adrian moving around."

"The defendant in this case?"

"Yes."

"Now, why didn't you mention earlier that you had seen this defendant . . ."

"Oh, just a minute, Your Honor," Mason interposed suavely. "This is an attempt to cross-examine his own witness. Apparently he's trying to impeach him."

"I'm inclined to think that objection is well-taken," Judge Norwood ruled.

"Oh, Your Honor, I'm simply trying to clarify the situation. If I don't go into it, Perry Mason is going to on cross-examination."

"Well, that's the proper place for it, on cross-examination," Judge Norwood said.

"What makes you think I'm going into it?" Mason asked the district attorney.

"Because, of course, you are. Don't be silly."

"I'm not silly," Mason said. "I don't see any reason at the moment for asking him why he didn't make any statement before about having seen the defendant. I'm not even certain that you asked him—did you ask him if he had seen the defendant?"

The district attorney hesitated.

"*Did* you ask him if he had seen the defendant?" Mason asked.

"I'm not on the witness stand," the district attorney said. "Ask the witness."

"Did the district attorney ever ask you if you had seen the defendant over there?" Mason asked.

"I object to that question as being out of order. I haven't finished with my direct examination yet."

"There you are," Mason said. "You invited me to ask him the question."

"I didn't invite you to. I challenged you to."

"Well, you told me to ask him the question, and I asked him the question. Now what are you kicking about?"

"That will do, gentlemen," Judge Norwood said, smiling. "I think the district attorney's invitation or challenge, or whatever it was, certainly could be deemed to be an invitation to cross-examine at least on that point. The objection is overruled.

"Mr. Burris, you have been asked whether the district attorney asked you if you had seen Mrs. Adrian over there."

"No, he didn't," Burris said. "If he had I'd have told him, but he didn't ask so I didn't tell him.

"I'd made up my mind I'd tell the truth if I was ever asked the question, but I wasn't going to volunteer the information. Mrs. Adrian's a neighbor of mine. She may have been over there, but she wasn't the one who killed Arthur Cushing, and I don't think she was the one who screamed. She was . . ."

"Never mind what you think," the district attorney snapped.

"Yes, sir," Burris said.

"No further cross-examination—at this time," Mason said.

The district attorney pounced back on the hapless witness. "Then what did you do after you recognized Mrs. Adrian?"

"Well, I talked it over with my wife and we decided . . ."

"I'm asking you what you *did*."

"Well, that's what I did. I talked. You asked me and I told you."

There was a ripple of merriment in the courtroom.

"Never mind the conversation. Just go ahead. What did you do? Where did you go?"

"I went over to the Cushing cottage."

"Why did you go over there?"
"To see if anything was wrong."
"What did you find?"
"I found the window smashed. I found the glass from the mirror smashed and all over the window sill, glass smashed all over the room on the inside, and some pieces of glass on the outside. I found Arthur Cushing sitting in a wheel chair all slumped over to one side, just like an inert sack of meal. There was blood on the front of his shirt, and I ran out and called the sheriff."
"Did you notice any tracks?"
"Not then I didn't."
"And after you had summoned the sheriff you were taken back to the scene of the crime?"
"No. I went back home. The sheriff told me to."
"And the sheriff roped off a place, didn't he, so there would be no confusion of tracks?"
"I saw the roped-off place after it got light. . . . I went over there then and the sheriff asked me some more questions."
"What tracks did you see there then, aside from yours and the sheriff's?"
"The tracks of a woman coming from the direction of the Adrian cottage."
"The sheriff asked you if you knew whose tracks those were, and you told him you didn't know. Isn't that right?"
"Yes."
"Why did you lie to him?"
"I didn't lie."
"You had *seen* Mrs. Belle Adrian, the defendant, there; therefore you knew those must be her tracks, yet you told the sheriff who was then investigating the murder that you didn't know whose tracks they were."
"That's right. I didn't know. I still don't know, and I doubt if you know either."
The courtroom echoed laughter at Sam Burris' rally. The Judge called for order and admonished the spectators.
"You knew Mrs. Adrian had been there?"

"Yes."

"How did you think she got there—by flying?"

"Objected to," Mason said perfunctorily, "as an attempt to cross-examine his own witness."

"Sustained."

"At that time, when you returned with the sheriff, you also saw the tracks of a woman coming from the direction of the road?"

"There were small tracks. I ain't saying for sure they were women's tracks, and I don't know where they came from. They may have gone from the house and then back to the house, for all I know. If you ask me, there's something funny about one set of those tracks."

"What was funny about it?"

"I don't really mean funny. I mean they just didn't look natural somehow, and I've done a right smart lot of tracking in my time. . . . *I* don't believe those tracks were ever made by . . . ."

"Never mind your conclusions," the district attorney interrupted coldly. "I am only asking for facts."

"Your Honor," Mason objected, "this gets more and more like a cross-examination."

Judge Norwood nodded. "I think so, too. Counsel will refrain from cross-examining his own witness."

"He's a hostile witness," Hale said.

"Nevertheless, he's your witness. You may ask leading questions if necessary because of his hostility, but don't try to cross-examine him, and don't try to browbeat him."

"I wasn't browbeating him."

"I don't think you were, but you were getting close to the line. The Court is warning you. Proceed with your questions."

"There were no tracks leading to the house other than those you have just mentioned?"

"Not that I could see."

"When you first reached the Cushing cottage did you notice the broken mirror from a compact? That is, small slivers of silvered glass?"

"No, sir."

"Did you notice any powder on the clothing of the deceased; that is, face powder such as might have come from a compact?"

"I didn't take no particular notice, no."

"You saw the frame of the mirror?"

"Yes. The smashed wooden frame with some fragments of glass still in it."

"There was no automobile parked at the place?"

"No, sir."

"Were there automobile tracks?"

"There was one set of automobile tracks. I didn't see 'em then. I saw these after daylight. It was an automobile that had been put in there before the frost had started to form, and then it went out after the frost formed. It just left one set of tracks going out."

"Anything else that you saw that first time?"

"I don't think I noticed too much. When I walked in and saw the setup I became all goose pimples. I figured the woman who had been with him for dinner had gone home, and . . ."

"What caused you to figure she had gone home?"

"I don't believe I can tell you, offhand. . . . Maybe I didn't have anything to go on, come to think of it. . . . But I think there was something that made me . . ."

"Never mind what you *think*," Hale interposed. "Tell us what you *saw*."

"Well, that's what I was trying to do. Seems to me there was a drinking glass with lipstick on it. . . ."

"Do you mean that you examined the drinking glass that had been broken on the floor?" Hale asked.

"No, I didn't examine the glass on the floor. I'm not too sure . . . Well, maybe there was a tumbler on the floor, and some moving-picture stuff in the living room. To tell you the truth, I'm pretty hazy about what was there and what wasn't. The front door was locked with a spring lock. I went around to the back. That door was unlocked and when I walked in and crossed the kitchen to this den the first thing I saw was that body all slumped down in the wheel chair and blood dripping down to the floor. . . . I remember that broken tumbler now. I saw red on it. Guess it must have been blood. I didn't go near it, but it looked red and I thought at the time it was lipstick."

"What was the position of the wheel chair?"

"Out about six or eight feet away from the window, turned so that the back was quartering toward the window."

"Now, immediately after you had notified the authorities you went back to your house, and then about daylight you went somewhere else. You went to see Mrs. Adrian, didn't you?"

"Objected to," Mason said. "Incompetent, irrelevant, immaterial."

"I'm trying to show the attitude, the bias of this witness."

"For the purposes of cross-examination?" Mason asked.

"I think the Court is entitled to take it into consideration," Hale said.

Mason said, "You keep trying to cross-examine your own witness. Don't do it. However, I'll stipulate he did go to see Mrs. Adrian."

"Just a moment, gentlemen," Judge Norwood said. "I have cautioned Counsel about these exchanges of repartee. Now, as I understand it, the question and the stipulation relate to what he did *after* he had discovered the body, after he had called the authorities, and after he had been told to go home and wait?"

"That's right. Yes, sir. For the purpose of showing bias. I am not going to try to defend the conduct of this witness, Your Honor. He has suppressed information which should have been given to us. I am not even going to point out that his motives in doing so were those of a man who was trying to be neighborly and constructive. I will state frankly to Counsel that I am not going to interpose any objections to Counsel's cross-examination of this witness. I suppose that Mr. Mason will literally tear him limb from limb. However, it is something Sam Burris has brought on himself."

"Are you entirely finished with your argument to the Court?" Mason asked.

"I was merely pointing out to the Court that I cannot condone this conduct in a witness; that while I know you're going to tear him to pieces and probably insinuate that he was planning blackmail later on, and all of these other things, I am not going to hold any brief for him. I turn the witness over to you for cross-examination."

Mason yawned ostensibly, then patted back the yawn with four polite fingers. "A very nice speech, Counselor," he said casually. "I suppose it makes you feel better. I have no questions of this witness."

"What?" Ives shouted incredulously.

Mason merely smiled.

Darwin Hale, the district attorney, looked at Mason with the expression one would reserve for a man who has suddenly taken leave of his senses. "No questions?"

"No."

"No questions whatever?"

"Not a single question."

Judge Norwood said, "That is all, Mr. Burris. You may leave the stand."

Darwin Hale seemed completely confused. He held a brief, whispered consultation with the special prosecutor, then said, "I'm sorry, Your Honor, in view of the developments, we had anticipated that there would be a cross-examination of this witness which would consume a large part of the afternoon, I . . ."

"Are you prepared to go ahead with your case?" Mason asked.

"I would like a brief ten-minute recess, Your Honor."

"Very well," Judge Norwood said. "I think that request is reasonable. Court will take a ten-minute recess."

As the Judge left the bench Mason felt Belle Adrian's trembling fingers on his arm.

"Mr. Mason," she whispered, "what must you think of me?"

"I think you're a fool," Mason said, shortly and crisply.

"Any person who hires an attorney, then lets the attorney prepare a case according to a false conception, is acting the part of a fool. . . . Did you know that Sam Burris had seen you?"

"Yes, he told me."

"When he came to call on you that Sunday morning?"

"Yes."

"Did he try to blackmail you?"

"What do you mean?"

"Did he want money to keep quiet?"

"Good heavens, no. He said he was doing it as a matter of neighborly accommodation."

Mason said, "He may have been. On the other hand, he might have come to you and asked for cash after you had been bound over and before trial before a jury. You are a little fool to let yourself get caught in that sort of a trap."

"Now what's going to happen?" she asked.

"Now," Mason said, "we stand about one chance in a thousand. . . . Now, at least be frank with me. Tell me what you did."

She said, "I didn't know Carlotta was home. I looked in the garage. The garage was empty, so I took it for granted she was still over at Arthur Cushing's house. I went out to the kitchen and looked out of the kitchen window over toward Cushing's house. I saw there were lights on and then I heard a woman scream. It was a scream of sheer terror, and I thought that it must be Carlotta."

"So you dressed and went over there?"

"I just jumped into some clothes and dashed over."

"What did you find?"

"I got in the house and found Arthur Cushing dead. I found Carlotta's broken compact on the floor, and . . . Well, I did what any mother would have done. I picked it up and put it in my pocket, then I looked around to see if there was any other incriminating evidence."

"Was there any?"

"I don't know. I didn't take any chances. I wiped places where there might have been fingerprints. I washed three tumblers and put them in the cupboard. I wiped fingerprints from bottles and put them away. I even rubbed a handkerchief over the doorknobs."

Mason groaned. "In your desire to help Carlotta, you undoubtedly obliterated the very evidence which might have cleared her."

Mrs. Adrian nodded dispiritedly, and, seeing that listless nod, Mason said, "You really think Carlotta must have killed him, don't you?"

"No. I did for a while. I don't now. . . . She thinks I killed him."

Mason said, "Tell me truthfully, did you walk down to Carlotta's automobile?"

"Mr. Mason, I give you my word, I did not."

"All right," Mason said, "if you're telling the truth now, we'll . . ."

"I give you my solemn assurance, Mr. Mason, that I am now telling you the absolute truth. I wouldn't have lied to you if it hadn't been for trying to save Carlotta, but I tried to spare her as much as possible. . . . And, of course, my strategy has backfired. She's now in a mess."

"You're the one who's in a mess now," Mason said. "All right, sit tight and we'll do the best we can."

Chapter 18

As court reconvened, Darwin Hale, who had apparently carefully planned a strategy, said, "Your Honor, I wish to recall the sheriff to the stand for just one more question or two."

"Very well."

Sheriff Elmore, back on the stand, testified briefly to having made a detailed examination of the automobile which Carlotta Adrian had driven on the night of the murder.

"You went over it carefully?"

"I did. Yes, sir."

"And did you examine the left front tire?"

"Yes, sir."

"That was the tire that was flat?"

"It was."

"Did you find what had caused the tire to go flat?"

"I did. Yes, sir."

"What was it?"

"Objected to," Mason said casually. "Incompetent, irrelevent and immaterial. No proper foundation laid."

"As to the first part of the objection, I will connect it up," the district attorney said. "On the ground that there is no proper foundation laid, I consider that's absurd."

"I don't," Mason retorted. "You're asking for the conclusion of the witness. You haven't qualified him as an expert. He can testify as to what he found in the tire and then you can have some expert tire man state whether or not that object would have caused the tire to go flat."

"Bosh!" Darwin Hale said. "That, Your Honor, is simply the desperate attempt of a drowning man to clutch at a straw.

I think when the Court hears the testimony the Court will realize the utter absurdity of the objection."

"I will overrule the objection," Judge Norwood said.

"What caused the tire to go flat?"

"A jagged piece of glass."

"Do you have that glass with you?"

"Yes, sir."

"Where did you find it?"

"I found it embedded in the casing of the tire in such a position that it had gone completely through the casing and was responsible for the cut in the inner tube, which had caused the tire to go flat."

Hale said, "I offer this piece of glass, Your Honor, as People's Exhibit E."

"No objection," Mason said.

"Cross-examine," Hale snapped.

"Now, then, Sheriff," Mason said, "you found this piece of glass in the tire?"

"Yes, sir."

"And you recognize that as being a piece of glass similar in appearance to that which came from the broken mirror?"

"Yes, sir."

"And did you make a spectroscopic analysis to determine whether it was the same glass?"

"I didn't do that myself, and this time it wasn't done in my presence. However, I know it was done."

"And the results indicated it was a piece of glass from that broken mirror?"

"Yes, sir."

"Did you dust the car for fingerprints?"

"Yes, sir. We examined, I think, every inch of that car."

"What fingerprints did you find?"

"We found fingerprints of the defendant, we found fingerprints of Carlotta, and we found a few fingerprints which had probably been there for some time and which couldn't be readily identified."

"Any that hadn't been there for some time?"

"Well, of course, it's hard to say," the sheriff said.

"You have a fingerprint expert in your office?"

"No, sir. In a county of this size I cannot afford one. I know a little something about fingerprints, and I have deputies who have done some work with fingerprints, but I wouldn't say that we had what you would call a fingerprint expert."

"Who developed these latent prints?"

"We developed some of them, but an expert technician was hired from the city. He came up and did much of the work."

"Now, then, let's get back to some of these unidentified prints you found."

"Oh, Your Honor," the district attorney said, "I don't think that's proper cross-examination. That's certainly going far afield."

"The sheriff stated he examined the car very carefully and I intend to show what he did and what he found," Mason said. "That's proper cross-examination."

"The objection is overruled."

"I want to find out something about the fingerprints that weren't classified, that weren't readily identified. Were there any fingerprints that impressed you as having been made recently, Sheriff?"

"Well . . . Yes, there was a print on the left-hand door-handle of the automobile which seemed to have been freshly made."

"A latent fingerprint?"

"That's right."

"It was developed to a point of visibility by dusting with powder?"

"Yes, sir."

"And photographed?"

"Yes, sir."

Mason said, "Do you have a photograph of that fingerprint?"

"I have. Yes, sir."

"Let's take a look at it."

"Oh, Your Honor," Hale said, "this is certainly not proper

cross-examination. If Mr. Mason wants to make the sheriff his own witness, let him do so, but I certainly object to having this brought out in this manner on cross-examination."

"I think it's proper," Judge Norwood said, obviously interested. "That fingerprint might be exceedingly important. The Court would like to take a look at it."

Sheriff Elmore reached in his inside coat pocket and pulled out an envelope. From the envelope he took a photograph and handed it to Perry Mason.

"Well," Mason said, "this is interesting. It seems to be a very clear-cut fingerprint."

"I believe that it is unusually clear," the sheriff said, "due probably to the fact that the thumb was pressed firmly against the metal of the door and left a very clear latent fingerprint."

Mason said, "I'd like to introduce this, Your Honor, as Defendant's Exhibit No. 1."

"No objection," Hale said wearily. "My only reason for objecting was that I didn't want to take up a lot of time with extraneous matters. It is not the fingerprint of the defendant, and it's not the fingerprint of her daughter, Carlotta. We don't know whose fingerprint it is. We don't much care."

Mason said, "Now, Sheriff, you stated that the sliver of glass had caused the puncture in the tire."

"Yes, sir."

"What makes you think it did?"

"Why, it stands to reason."

"You aren't an expert, are you?"

"Well, I've driven a car and I've had enough flat tires to blame near make me an expert," the sheriff blurted.

Mason waited until the burst of laughter in the courtroom had subsided before he said, "You never repaired tires for a living?"

"No, sir. Certainly not."

"And when you have had flat tires your practice has been to jack up the car, put on a spare tire, and take the punctured tire to a tire shop to be repaired?"

"Yes, sir."

"How did it happen then that you considered yourself expert enough to try to tell what caused the puncture in the tire that was on this front wheel?"

"This was something I couldn't very well delegate," the sheriff said. "I had the tire removed in my presence, and then when we saw a jagged tear in the tube I ran my hand on the inside of the casing to find what had caused that tear. I actually cut the back of my hand on this fragment of glass which was protruding through the inside casing of the tire, and I cut into the casing and removed it."

"You cut into the casing?"

"I cut a hole out of the casing so that I could remove this piece of glass virtually intact."

"A sliver of glass," Mason said, "about an inch and a half long, wedge-shaped like a small piece of pie, coming to a very sharp, chiseled edge?"

"Yes, sir. Stuck straight into the tread—right angles."

"Now, then, did you study the tracks to see how long the automobile had been operated on a flat tire?"

"Yes, sir. We could tell that the tire had been flat almost from the very moment it had been driven away from the Cushing cottage.

"I will state further, Mr. Mason, that there was only one set of automobile tracks near the Cushing cottage. Those tracks were made by a car which had been driven away from the cottage after the frost had formed, and the tracks indicated that the left front tire had started to go flat within a very few feet. It had been driven for approximately a hundred yards with the tire getting more and more flat all the time, and then the car had been left."

"Thank you," Mason said suavely, "that's all."

"No further questions?" Judge Norwood asked.

"No further questions," Darwin Hale said, and then, apparently acting in accordance with a preconceived plan, stood up and said, "That, Your Honor, concludes our case. On that presentation we ask that the defendant be bound over to the Superior Court for trial."

Judge Norwood nodded. "I think there is evidence that a

crime has been committed, and there certainly is sufficient evidence to make it appear probable that the defendant . . ."

"Just a moment, Your Honor," Mason interrupted. "Aren't you going to give *me* a chance to put on *my* side of the case?"

Judge Norwood showed surprise. "You mean you are going to put the defendant on the stand?"

"I didn't say that," Mason said. "I said I wanted to put on a case."

"Very well," Judge Norwood said. "You'll pardon me, Counselor. I didn't want to foreclose the defendant. I had assumed, of course, in view of the showing in this case, that . . . well, ordinarily in this county there's not much of a contest on a preliminary, and particularly when the evidence is so overwhelmingly . . . However, I won't commit myself in advance, Mr. Mason. Go right ahead. Put on your defense."

"Very well," Mason said. "My first witness will be Marion Keats. Is Marion Keats in court?"

There was a swirl of activity in the back of the courtroom and Marion Keats, getting to her feet, came striding toward the witness chair.

From the fact that neither the district attorney nor C. Creston Ives even bothered to look around, Mason knew that she had been in touch with the district attorney and the special prosecutor.

He waited patiently while the witness was being sworn, and then said, "Your Honor, this is a hostile witness. I may have to ask leading questions. I . . ."

"How do *we* know she's hostile?" Darwin Hale asked.

"Look at her," Mason said, smiling.

"Go ahead with your questions," Judge Norwood said.

"Your name is Marion Keats?"

"Yes."

"Miss or Mrs.?"

"I . . . I have been married."

"Keats was the name of your husband?"

"Yes."

"Do you go by the name of Mrs. Marion Keats or Miss Marion Keats?"

"I go by the name of Miss Marion Keats. I guess I have a right to take any name I want to."

"Quite all right," Mason said. "I was only asking the question."

"Well, I answered it."

"Now, you were acquainted with Arthur Cushing in his lifetime?"

"Yes."

"You occasionally went skiing with him?"

"Yes."

"You were in Bear Valley on the night of the second and the morning of the third?"

"I was here on the morning of the third," she answered, her mouth a straight line of angry indignation.

"And you were, I believe, also at the funeral of Arthur B. Cushing?"

"Objected to. Incompetent, irrelevant and immaterial," C. Creston Ives said.

"Sustained."

"You had been skiing with Arthur Cushing on several occasions?"

"Yes."

"How long had you known him?"

"About six months."

Suddenly, without warning, Mason jumped up from his chair, took two steps toward the witness, pointed his forefinger at her face and shouted, "Let's hear you scream!"

The witness, sucking in her breath, gave a quick exclamation of startled surprise.

Darwin Hale and C. Creston Ives were both on their feet, both talking at once.

"Order!" Judge Norwood shouted. "Order in the court! One at a time now, gentlemen. What is it, Mr. Hale?"

"Incompetent, irrelevant and immaterial!" Hale spluttered. "An attempt to bully, browbeat and intimidate his own witness."

C. Creston Ives cut in with cold, academic precision. "If the object of this questioning is to lay a trap for his own witness, Your Honor, it is improper examination. If it is for the purpose of making a test to try to identify this witness by her scream, something which Your Honor will admit is a hopeless impossibility, the test must be performed under the conditions which would be comparable to those which existed at the time."

"Let's hear your scream!" Mason repeated again.

The witness bared her teeth and before anyone could stop her gave vent to a hoarse, inarticulate scream of rage and hatred, an animal-like cry in which there was no note of terror, only anger.

"Thank you," Mason said, smiling and bowing. "Thank you very much indeed, Miss Keats."

There was a puzzled silence which permeated the courtroom.

"Quite apparently," Judge Norwood said dryly, "the witness, a rather high-strung, emotional young woman, has seen fit not to wait for the ruling of the Court. The objection, therefore, becomes moot.

"You may proceed, Mr. Mason."

"Do I *have* to put up with any more of this?" Marion Keats asked the Judge.

"You are a witness," Judge Norwood said. "Counsel will ask you questions. You only have to answer pertinent questions. Opposing Counsel and the Court will see that your rights are protected. If you had remained patient and quiet, I was about to sustain the objection."

"I'm sorry, Your Honor, but I'm emotionally upset. I'd like to have an opportunity to consult a lawyer before I answer any more questions. This is all part of a blackmailing campaign to smear my reputation. Mr. Mason virtually said as much when he subpoenaed me. I think I'm entitled to have an attorney. I have been told a lawyer can't use the writs of a court just to drag someone who doesn't know anything about the case into the limelight."

Hale nudged Ives and grinned.

Judge Norwood said, "You are quite right in your general understanding of the law. A person who knows any facts which are pertinent is obliged to be a witness when called, but one cannot be dragged into court merely for the purpose of . . . Well, I will refrain from further comment at this time.

"Mr. Mason, do you have anything to say?"

"If she wants a lawyer, let her get one," Mason said.

"Very well, you are now excused," Judge Norwood said to Marion Keats. "Consult a lawyer and return here tomorrow morning at ten o'clock, bringing your lawyer with you if you see fit.

"Do you have another witness you can call, Mr. Mason?"

"I'd like to close my case, Your Honor, but there are certain technical matters on which the prosecution has left very large gaps, bits of evidence which the district attorney has apparently deemed it necessary to omit."

"What do you mean?" Hale demanded. "I haven't omitted anything."

"Oh, yes, you have," Mason said. "You haven't introduced the wheel chair in which the body was found."

"I have introduced evidence as to all pertinent facts concerning that wheel chair. It is, of course, rather big and bulky, and for that reason I saw no reason for . . ."

"Exactly," Mason interposed. "The wheel chair is one of the most important bits of circumstantial evidence in this case, yet the district attorney has contented himself with having the sheriff testify that there was no glass ground into the rubber tires of the wheel chair."

"Oh, all right," Hale said. "I'll yield to Counsel's whim. If he wants the wheel chair in evidence he can have it . . . Sheriff, bring in that wheel chair, will you?"

"You're now asking to reopen your case?" Mason asked.

"That's right. I'll reopen it. I'll bring in the wheel chair and have it introduced in evidence."

"Very well," Mason said.

The sheriff brought the wheel chair from an exhibit room in the back of the courtroom.

"This is it," he said.

"Do you want the sheriff to get on the stand to swear to that?" Hale asked.

Mason shrugged his shoulders. "If you say it's the wheel chair I'll stipulate that it may be received in evidence."

"That's all," Hale said.

Mason said, "I now wish to call Sam Burris as my witness."

"As *your* witness?" Hale said, surprised.

"That's right."

"Very well," Judge Norwood said. "Mr. Burris, you'll take the stand as witness for the defense. You've already been sworn to testify in this case so you won't need to be sworn again. Go ahead, Mr. Mason."

Mason indicated the bloodstained wheel chair in the courtroom near the witness stand.

"Mr. Burris, as nearly as you can tell, this is the wheel chair in which the body of Arthur Cushing was sitting when you entered the Cushing cottage on the early morning of the third?"

"Yes, sir."

"You don't see anything about that chair now that looks any different to you from the way it was when you saw it then?"

"No, sir."

"Mr. Burris, were you sitting right here in court a few minutes ago and did you hear the witness Marion Keats scream?"

"I didn't hear her scream," Burris said. "I heard her give sort of a funny little cry. It wasn't what I'd call a scream.

"Mr. Mason, I've been wondering if you tried to make that woman scream so I could identify her. I can tell you right now that there wasn't any sound she made here in the courtroom that sounded at all like the scream I heard."

"I want to get it straight," Mason said. "As I understand it, there was no scream when you heard the mirror being thrown at Arthur Cushing?"

Hale leaped to his feet. "Don't answer that, don't answer that," he shouted at the witness, and then, turning to the

Court, said, "Your Honor, I object. This is not proper examination of the witness. It assumes a fact not in evidence. It calls for the conclusion of the witness, and it assumes a condition directly contrary to what actually happened.

"Counsel knows that the mirror was not thrown by any woman, or any other person at Arthur Cushing. That mirror was thrown by Arthur Cushing in a last desperate effort at self-defense, and then he was shot."

"Well, without going into the merits of the various contentions," Judge Norwood said, "I think I will sustain the objection on the ground that it calls for a conclusion of the witness. He can state as to when he heard the scream with reference to the time he heard the crash of the breaking glass."

"All right," Mason said cheerfully. "I'll reframe my question. *When* did you hear the sound of the scream with reference to the sound of the breaking glass, Mr. Burris?"

Sam Burris hesitated. "It's sort of hard," he said, "to get things straightened out in your mind when you're waking up out of a sleep."

"I understand," Mason said sympathetically. "Just do the best you can, Mr. Burris."

"Well," Burris said, "I think, the way I remember it, I heard the sound of breaking glass, then I heard a shot, and then I sort of lay there, half-asleep, and it was quite some time later that we heard a woman scream."

"Now, how long were you lying there half-asleep?"

"Oh, a few seconds maybe."

"As much as a minute?"

"It could have been more than a minute."

"As much as five minutes?"

Burris was thoughtful. "Yes," he said, "as much as five minutes. I'll be frank with you, Mr. Mason, I might have sort of dozed off—but not for long. I'll put an extreme limit on it. I'll say that perhaps . . . Well, I don't know."

Mason said, "You were going to put an extreme limit on it, Mr. Burris. What caused you to change your mind?"

"Well, it didn't sound reasonable. It couldn't have been reasonable."

"In other words," Mason said, "to be perfectly frank, you don't *know* how long an interval there was between the sound of the breaking glass and the scream, but when you try to put an extreme limit on it you reach a conclusion which seems to you to be absurd in view of the facts. Is that right?"

"I object to the question on the ground that it's argumentative," Hale said. "Further on the ground that it's an attempt to cross-examine his own witness. Mr. Mason made a very spectacular grandstand in passing up the cross-examination of this witness and . . ."

"The objection is highly technical, and will be overruled," Judge Norwood said. "Counsel seems to lose sight of the fact that the ultimate object of a hearing of this sort is to satisfy the Court, and not to enable Counsel to perform legal gymnastics in a courtroom, or to show their skill in leaping from one technicality to another. Go ahead and answer that question, Mr. Burris."

"Well, to tell you the truth," Burris said, "I *was* going to say that there might have been an interval of as much as fifteen minutes from the time I heard the shot and the crash of glass until I heard the scream. It just didn't sound reasonable to have it that way, but somehow or other I have a feeling that there might—there just might have been that much of an interval."

"And then you got up out of bed immediately when you heard the scream?" Mason said.

"Not exactly. I got up after I heard the glass break. Maybe it was two or three minutes. I stood there, but beyond the fact there were lights over at the Cushing cabin, I couldn't see a thing. I didn't use the telescope, not then, but I did wake up my wife—and then just about the time she was getting up we heard the scream."

Mason said, "You have no way of knowing yourself whether the sound of the breaking mirror and the crashing window were caused by someone throwing a mirror at Arthur Cushing and missing him, or by Arthur Cushing throwing a mirror at someone?''

''That's right.''

''Quite obviously,'' Hale said dryly, ''the answer speaks for itself. It is quite obvious to the prosecution that the mirror was thrown by Mr. Cushing in a last desperate effort to defend himself.''

''Then he must have thrown it backwards,'' Mason said.

''It is the contention of the prosecution, Your Honor,'' Hale said, ''that the mirror was thrown by Mr Cushing at some assailant who was, at that time, between him and the window; that, having thrown the mirror, Mr. Cushing pivoted his chair, trying to keep his face turned toward his assailant, and that was when the fatal shot was fired.''

''I think I understand the prosecution's contention,'' Judge Norwood said.

''I thought you said the chair wasn't moved,'' Mason observed.

''It wasn't moved after all that glass got on the floor.''

''And all the glass must have got on the floor immediately after the mirror was thrown.''

''It may have been on the floor, but it was kicked around the place after Cushing was shot. I think the Court and I understand the situation perfectly.''

''I'm not sure that we do,'' Judge Norwood said, frowning and scratching his head above the temples. ''Mr. Mason opens up an interesting field of speculation.''

''Which I will endeavor to develop a little further,'' Mason said cheerfully. ''Mr. Burris, would you mind sitting over in the wheel chair in just about the position Mr. Cushing was when you saw the body.''

The witness got in the wheel chair and slumped down listlessly.

''Now,'' Mason said, ''without moving anything except the position of your shoulders and head, please straighten in the chair. I want you to keep your hips and feet in exactly the position in which they were a moment ago.''

Burris obediently straightened.

Mason handed the antique mirror to Burris. "Now," he said, "the wheel chair was about six feet from the window that had been broken?"

"That's right."

Mason said, "The corner of the Judge's bench over there is about six feet away. Let's see if you can throw that mirror and hit the corner of the Judge's bench with it."

"Just a moment! Just a moment!" the district attorney shouted, jumping to his feet. "That's not a condition under which a test can be made."

Judge Norwood said, "The Court certainly doesn't intend to have mirrors smashed around this courtroom."

"He can't throw the mirror that far from a sitting position in the wheel chair," Mason said, "and he's a stronger, more husky man than Arthur Cushing was. If he raises his arms and puts them far enough back so he can throw that mirror for a distance of six feet while he's in a sitting position in the wheel chair, the chair will go over backward. He can't throw it that far. Neither could Arthur Cushing have thrown it."

"Cushing *did* throw it," Hale said. "He must have."

"Go ahead and try to throw it," Mason said to the witness.

Burris raised the mirror. A puzzled expression came over his face.

"Let *me* try that," Judge Norwood said.

He left the bench, sat in the wheel chair, raised the heavy mirror, put his arms back, hastily lowered them. "Have you tried this?" he asked the district attorney.

"No, Your Honor."

"Better try it then," Judge Norwood said, tersely, returning to the bench.

"But, Your Honor, the mirror *was* thrown," Hale insisted.

"Not by anyone sitting in that wheel chair," the Judge said positively; "not any six feet. That mirror must weigh thirty pounds."

"But, Your Honor," Hale said with exasperation, "I dislike to be drawn into an argument with the Court, but if Your

Honor will only look squarely at all of the evidence, you will see that it is a manifest impossibility for anyone to have thrown that mirror at Arthur Cushing."

"Well, it was a manifest impossibility for him to have got in that wheel chair and thrown *that* mirror any six feet," Judge Norwood said.

"But it wasn't *that* mirror which was thrown, Your Honor. The Court will remember that we strenuously objected to the manner in which *this* mirror was brought into the case. Perry Mason adroitly insinuated it by asking a witness if this mirror was *about* the same size and of *about* the same weight."

Judge Norwood nodded. "However," he pointed out, "the mirror which was thrown obviously isn't available for an experiment of this sort, and it must have been a heavy mirror. A man in a wheel chair might have held it in his lap and *tossed* it, but he didn't raise his arms back over his head and *throw* it.

"Now, Miss Keats wishes to consult Counsel and the Court wants to inspect the premises where the crime is alleged to have been committed. So we'll take a recess until tomorrow morning at ten o'clock."

As the spectators moved out of the courtroom, Paul Drake slipped close to Perry Mason and said, "There's something that's not so good, Perry. It seems Marion Keats went to the district attorney's office as soon as she arrived. He fixed it all up for her to get on the stand, answer a few questions and then ask for a chance to see a lawyer.

"It's all cooked up. She's to go to a guy named Lansing, who is generally a pain in the neck, one of those sticklers for ethics. He's going to accuse you of abusing the process of the court and charge you didn't expect to prove a thing by Marion Keats, but were just trying to insinuate an undue intimacy with Cushing so as to take the heat off your client.

"They're going to try to make a serious charge against you."

Mason's jaw tightened.

"I had an idea it was all fixed up, Paul. Neither Ives nor Hale even bothered to look around when I called her and she started toward the stand. I knew then they'd cooked up something."

"Can they do that?" Della Street asked.

"If they can prove I didn't have anything in particular for her to testify to, they can be disagreeable," Mason admitted.

"Well, they're going to be *very* disagreeable," Paul Drake said. "And for your information, Perry, Judge Norwood is rabid on the subject of abusing judicial process, and the lawyer they've picked out for Miss Keats is a stuffed shirt who is always carping about ethics and asking for disciplinary action."

Mason frowned. "I'll admit I took a desperate chance, Paul. I thought that she'd come around to beg for mercy before she'd ever go on the stand. Then I thought I'd either get information or tell her she didn't need to be in court; that I'd excuse her. Now I'm in a jam unless I can show I had *some* reason to believe she could testify to some specific and pertinent fact."

"She'd have begged you for a break if it hadn't been for the district attorney and Ives," Drake said. "She went to them and they saw a chance to roast you on the grid."

Mason narrowed his eyes. "Get busy on that fingerprint, Paul. If we can't get *something* I'm in a bad jam. . . . I'll try to bluff my way out, but these fellows are all part of a local clique. . . . Get busy, Paul."

Chapter 19

Della Street's assistant at the suite in the hotel greeted Mason, Della Street and Paul Drake on their return from court.

"George Henry Lansing telephoned," she said. "He's an attorney. He wants you to get in touch with him right away. He says it's exceedingly important. It's about Marion Keats."

"Oh, yes," Mason said. "I'd like to talk with him. Get him on the phone for me."

A moment later, when the girl nodded, Mason picked up the telephone, said, "Hello," and heard a dry, husky voice speaking in terms of measured deliberation. "Mr. Mason, I have been retained by Marion Keats, whom you have subpoenaed as a witness for the defense in the case of People versus Adrian."

"Uh-huh," Mason said.

"I wish to tell you that I consider the subpoena was very ill-advised."

"I'll judge my own subpoenas," Mason said. "What else do you want to tell me?"

"I feel you should be notified that it will be far better for you to close your case without any further attempts to cross-examine Miss Keats."

"Indeed," Mason said.

"If you force her to go on the stand again, I will be there as her attorney. I shall object to your using her purely for the purpose of a fishing expedition. I shall insist that her right of privacy is to be protected. I will state to the Court that I feel you have abused the process of the court, and if it becomes necessary as a last resort I shall advise the witness not to answer any questions, and I intend to prefer charges against you."

"Anything else?" Mason asked cheerfully.

"That is all," Lansing said, "and that is final."

"*You* think it's final," Mason told him. "You have your client in court tomorrow morning or I'll have her cited for contempt."

"She will be there, but at that time I will ask to have her excused from the subpoena, and I will further make a formal charge that you have abused the process of the court."

"Has your client told you everything?" Mason asked.

"Certainly."

"All right," Mason said, "since you're throwing your weight around and making threats, how would you like to be charged with suppressing evidence, obstructing justice, and becoming an accomplice after the fact?"

"You can't threaten me, Mr. Mason."

"The hell I can't," Mason said. "You tried to threaten me, didn't you? Where are you now?"

"I'm in my office."

"Where's that?"

"In the Equitable Bank Building."

"That's directly across from the hotel, isn't it?"

"Yes, sir."

"Sit right there," Mason said. "I'm coming over."

"I would not be convenient for me to see you at the present moment. I . . ."

"If you don't see me," Mason said, "you'll be the sorriest individual that ever walked out of a courtroom."

"Mr. Mason, I warn you that I cannot permit my client to be browbeaten or bullied, nor do I intend to . . ."

"Stay right where you are," Mason said. "I'll be there in three minutes."

He slammed up the telephone, grabbed his hat, said to Della Street and Paul Drake, "Wait here. I may be calling you."

He dashed out of the hotel room, disdained the somewhat antiquated elevator and took the stairs two at a time, pell-melled out through the lobby, crossed the street, entered the office of the Equitable Bank Building and found that George Henry Lansing had his offices on the third floor.

Mason went up, saw the door marked "Entrance" and barged in.

A somewhat flustered secretary said, "Are you Mr. Mason? Well, Mr. Lansing is busy at the moment, but . . ."

"Tell Mr. Lansing," Mason said, "that I am here prepared to convince him his client is mixed up in a murder right up to her eyebrows. I'll give him ten seconds to decide whether he wants to hear about it now, or whether he wants to hear it in court tomorrow morning. And if it's the latter, I intend to show that I came to his office to tell him what I had in mind and to convince him his client is mixed up in the murder and he wouldn't listen. If he tries to claim I've abused the process of the court after that I'll rip him wide open.

"Now go tell him that and see how he reacts. If he's a slow thinker it may take a little time for it to soak in, so I'll make it thirty seconds. Go tell him."

She seemed undecided. "Mr. Lansing told me to explain to you that he was very busy and . . ."

"And you've explained it," Mason said. "I've given you a message to take to him. Are you going to take it?"

Without a word she turned and slipped discreetly through the door to the inner office.

Within some thirty seconds she was back, followed by a tall, cadaverous individual in the early fifties. He had high cheekbones, a bald head, a long neck, faded blue eyes, thin gray lips, and an air of funereal solemnity.

"How do you do, Mr. Mason? I felt that I should explain in person to you that, as attorney for Marion Keats, I have said all that I . . ."

Mason raised his voice. "I'm here to explain what I want Marion Keats to testify to. I don't want you to do anything except listen. When you see your client again, ask her how much she paid an informant to telephone her that Carlotta Adrian had a tête-à-tête dinner date with Arthur Cushing. Ask her where she was on the night of the murder, somewhere around two-thirty in the morning."

"Those are my client's private affairs," Lansing said. "She doesn't have to disclose her private affairs."

"All right," Mason said, raising his voice. "I've given her opportunity. I'll be willing to listen to explanations and spare her a lot of embarrassment if she'll talk frankly. Perhaps I can keep from putting her on the stand. If she . . ."

The door to Lansing's private office burst open. Marion Keats, white-faced, stood on the threshold, said, "Mr. Mason, if you'll let me explain . . ."

"Get back in that office," George Lansing ordered, without turning his head.

"I want to explain to Mr. Mason," Marion Keats said. "If he's found that out I . . ."

"He's bluffing," Lansing said. "Get back in the office."

Mason grinned. "I won't talk to your client, Lansing. That would be unethical. I'll talk to *you*. If your client would rather have all this stuff come out on the witness stand and be spread over the pages of the newspapers, that's her privilege. If you want to talk it over now, you can . . ."

"I have tried to explain to you, Mr. Mason, that my statement to you was complete, considered and final. I'm going to ask you to leave."

"Thanks," Mason said. "You're a slow thinker. It may take all night for it to soak in that I've pulled all the teeth out of your trap. I tried to tell you why I subpoenaed Marion Keats and you wouldn't listen. I offered you a chance to keep her off the stand and you refused to hear me but ordered me out of your office. Tell *that* to your friend, the district attorney."

Turning on his heel, Mason walked out of the office, leaving a badly nonplussed lawyer and a frightened, angry client behind him.

Back in the hotel, Drake and Della Street were waiting with poorly concealed anxiety.

"How'd you do, Perry?"

"I ran my best bluff. I knew she must have been in his private office when he telephoned. If he'd been a quick thinker he'd have rushed her out of there before I arrived.

"He's a slow thinker. He didn't do it. I sent his secretary in with a message I hoped would make Marion Keats insist on a conference.

"It worked with her, but he wouldn't fall for it. He's a guy with a one-track mind. When he starts for one objective he can't think of anything else."

"Is that bad—for you?" Drake asked.

"It's going to be bad unless we can turn up something before . . ."

The telephone rang sharply.

Drake answered it and a moment later hung up, turned to Mason and said, "This may help, Perry. You called the turn on that fingerprint. It's Nora Fleming's right thumbprint, and Sam Burris called up to say that Marion Keats is the young woman he told Mrs. Adrian about—the woman whom he'd seen at Arthur Cushing's cottage several times."

Chapter 20

As court reconvened in the morning, even standing room was at a premium.

"Proceed with the case," Judge Norwood said. "I believe this was the time fixed for continuing the examination of Miss Marion Keats as a witness for the defense."

Mason said, "That is right, Your Honor. I now wish to recall Marion Keats to the stand. I understand she has retained counsel to represent her."

George Lansing arose to his full height and said in his dry, husky voice, "Your Honor, I represent Miss Keats. I object to having her called as a witness, and I charge Defense Counsel with having abused the process of this court."

"In what way?" Judge Norwood asked.

"He has subpoenaed this witness purely in an effort to besmirch her character by making her a red herring for the sensational press. She knows nothing about this case, has no information that would be of the slightest value, but she does, however, have a background of friendship with the decedent. Predicating his actions entirely upon a fortuitous discovery of that background, Mr. Mason has sought a legalized blackmail of the defendant, seeking to crucify her upon the witness stand merely in order to furnish a diversion which will be pounced upon by the sensational press, thereby distracting attention from the predicament of Mr. Mason's client, the defendant."

Judge Norwood looked at Perry Mason with a puzzled frown. "That is a serious charge, Mr. Mason, coming as it does from so conservative and prominent a member of the Bar. I trust you are prepared to refute it."

"Put Miss Keats on the stand," Mason said. "Let me ask

her five questions and we'll very soon find out whether she knows anything about the case."

"Mr. Mason," Judge Norwood said, "I feel the Court should warn you at this time that *if* the statement made by Mr. Lansing is true, or *if* it can be established that such are the facts in the case, it will constitute a most serious charge. It might be in your own best interests to meet the charge and refute it *before* Miss Keats goes on the stand again."

"The charge has been made," Mason said. "It's serious. She has already been on the stand. Now the question is, am I to be convicted of misconduct simply on the strength of a charge made by an attorney?"

"No, no, certainly not," Judge Norwood said.

"Am I to be deprived of an opportunity to examine a witness on behalf of the defendant simply because . . . ?"

"Certainly not."

"Then," Mason said, "I want Miss Keats to take the stand once more."

"Of course," Darwin Hale interposed, "by these tactics Counsel is doing the very thing that my esteemed fellow member of the Bar accused him of doing, to wit, making a legalized red herring out of this witness."

"Just let me ask her five questions," Mason said. "You can go ahead and make your objections and let the Court rule on those objections. That's the orderly way to handle this thing."

"I was trying to caution Counsel for his own good, and prevent him from placing himself in a position where he would be subject to disciplinary action," Lansing said.

"Just take care of your own ethics and I'll take care of mine," Mason told him.

"What do you mean by that?"

"When did Miss Keats *first* consult you?"

"That's a matter of professional privilege."

"What *she* said and what *she* did are matters of privilege, but if *you* had arranged with her and with the district attorney to let her go on the stand pretending she knew nothing about her rights, and then ask the court for permission to consult counsel when as a matter of fact she had already consulted counsel, you'd better give this whole matter a little more thought."

"You know, I resent that," Lansing said.

"Don't resent it, deny it," Mason challenged.

Lansing rubbed his hand over his head, glanced at Hale, who was suddenly very busy pawing over papers, and said, "Very well, Miss Keats. If Counsel insists, take the stand."

Marion Keats glared at him. "But I thought you told me I wouldn't have to . . ."

"Take the stand," Lansing repeated. "I am laying the foundation for formal charges."

Angry and a little frightened, Marion Keats again walked forward to take her position on the witness stand.

"Now, Miss Keats," Lansing warned, "don't be in a hurry to answer questions, because the district attorney will object to *most* of these questions, and I will object to *all* of them. You will wait until after the Court has ruled upon each of these objections before you say anything. Then you probably won't have to answer at all. Don't be frightened by questions. I am here to protect your rights."

Mason said, "Miss Keats, you're acquainted with Nora Fleming, the housekeeper who was employed by the Cushings?"

"Objected to as incompetent, irrelevant and immaterial, having no bearing on the issues in this case," the district attorney said, quite evidently acting out part of a well-rehearsed, well-planned program which had been decided upon between him and Lansing.

"And as Miss Keats' attorney," Lansing added, "I will object on the ground that the question is merely a further attempt to abuse the process and power of the Court, that Counsel has no well-defined objective in mind, that he is merely on a fishing expedition, and that the sole purpose of this examination is to pillory the witness by showing a perfectly natural, normal friendship which she had with the dead man in a sinister light, and, by means of adroitly framed questions, placing the defendant in a false position before the public insofar as that relationship is concerned."

Mason said, "So far all the implications that there was anything wrong about that friendship have come from you."

Judge Norwood said, "Mr. Mason, the statement has been made that in using this witness you have no preconceived plan, no definite objective in mind; that charge is now formally before the Court on this objection."

"That statement," Mason said, "in common with many other statements that have been made here this morning, is completely erroneous. If Your Honor wishes, I will set forth my objectives, although I am well aware that in doing so I lose the element of surprise which I feel may be advantageous."

"Nevertheless," Judge Norwood said, "I think in view of the very serious accusations that have been made against you, Mr. Mason, you should perhaps state generally what your objective is."

"Very well, Your Honor. I expect to show by this witness that she was in love with Arthur Cushing, that Cushing was a man of rather inclusive fancies, was definitely not a one-woman man, and that the witness was insanely jealous.

"I expect to show that this witness made arrangements with Nora Fleming, the housekeeper, to telephone her the next time Arthur Cushing and Carlotta Adrian had a tête-à-tête date; that this witness intended to come up to the lake and confront them."

"Oh, Your Honor," Lansing interposed. "This is purest fancy, this is . . . invading the privacy of the witness. Now, by Counsel's own admission it appears he is contemplating doing the very thing . . ."

"The Court asked me to state my objectives and I'm stating them," Mason interposed, raising his voice. "You keep quiet until I've finished and then you can make any statement you want."

"I warn you that if you defame the character of this witness you . . ."

"You've warned me a dozen times," Mason said. "Now let me answer the Court's question."

Lansing, rather perplexed, looked at Darwin Hale in a vain hope that Hale would take some action.

Mason pitched his voice so that an interruption would have been drowned out. "About nine-twenty on the evening of the second, I expect to show that Nora Fleming, the housekeeper, having put dinner on the table, slipped out of the house, dashed over to a public pay station, rushed through a call to Marion Keats, and said one word and one word only into the telephone. She said, 'Yes,' and hung up.

"And I expect to show that Marion Keats understood what was meant by that mysterious telephone conversation which was in accordance with a prearranged scheme, that she jumped into her automobile, dashed here in the shortest possible time, and went to a prearranged meeting place where she was joined by Nora Fleming; that in driving along the road toward Arthur Cushing's house, they came upon the abandoned automobile of Carlotta Adrian standing by the side of the road; that either Marion Keats or Nora Fleming thereupon walked from Carlotta Adrian's automobile to the cottage of Arthur Cushing at about two-thirty in the morning and at approximately the time Sam Burris heard a woman scream."

"That's preposterous!" Lansing shouted. "It's a creation of your own fancy. There isn't a shred of evidence to substantiate such a claim. There is an even more flagrant abuse of the court's process than I had anticipated. There isn't in all the world a single shred of evidence to support these libelous, ridiculously absurd charges."

"And to prove it," Mason went on, as though he hadn't heard the interruption, "I will ask this witness how it happened that Nora Fleming left her right thumbprint on the handle of the door of Carlotta Adrian's car, and if the Court needs any more proof you can look at the face of Marion Keats and . . ."

"No!" Marion Keats screamed, jumping up from the witness stand. "Oh, no, you can't pin *that* on me! You can't do it. You can't do that to me! It was entirely an innocent action on my part. I walked into the place and found him dead. It was as much of a shock to me as . . ."

She abruptly ceased talking.

Mason smiled at Judge Norwood and said, "Now, Your Honor, in view of that statement from the witness, and in view of the proof I have offered, I will sit down and give Mr. George Henry Lansing an opportunity to argue to the Court that I am abusing the processes of the court, that I have no definite plan in mind and that this witness is to serve the function of being merely a legal red herring."

And Mason, acting as though he had no further interest in the proceedings, sat down.

Lansing kept stroking his bald head with the palm of his hand in a gesture of dazed futility.

"Well, Mr. Lansing?" Judge Norwood prompted.

"Your Honor, this comes as a complete surprise to me. I feel that the witness is hysterical, that she is overwrought, that she has been suffering mental tortures because of her knowledge that she was to be subjected to such an ordeal. I feel that her statement does not reflect the truth, but rather is the result of hysteria. I ask that the case be continued until she can consult a physician and . . ."

"The Court continued the case yesterday so she could consult an attorney."

"She needs a physician now, Your Honor."

"She may need something else," the Judge said. "The objection is overruled. Now, Mr. Mason, do you want to interrogate the witness?"

"I do."

"No, no," Marion Keats said. "I'll tell it! I'll tell everything! Just make that man leave me alone.

"Arthur Cushing was going to marry me, that is, he *said* he was. I guess he said the same thing to others. I thought he was playing around, so I made arrangements with Nora Fleming to call me the next time he was getting ready to put on the wolf act.

"She called me Saturday night. I drove up and met Nora Fleming. We started over to the Cushing cottage in my car. We came on Carlotta's stalled automobile—at least, we thought it was stalled at the time. I brought my car to a stop. Nora stepped from the running board of my car to the running board of Carlotta's car, then opened the door and said, 'The little minx couldn't have been gone more than a few minutes. The car's still warm.' Then she picked up this compact, saw the engraving on it, and said, 'Perhaps *this* will interest you.' "

"What compact?" Judge Norwood asked. "You can't mean the compact that . . ."

"That's exactly the one I *do* mean. It was an expensive compact. Gold, with a diamond set in it and engraving on it, 'Arthur to Carlotta with love.' "

"So what did you do?" Judge Norwood asked, his lips grim.

She said, "I was so mad I couldn't see straight. I knew then there was no chance to walk in and catch them necking. I took that compact and told Nora Fleming, 'You wait right there in the car, Nora. Don't move. I'm going to settle this myself.' It was only about seventy-five or a hundred yards over to Arthur's cottage, and I ran over there every step of the way."

"Then what did you do?"

"I had a key to the front door. Nora had given me her key to the door. That's one reason I needed her. I wanted naturally to get in without knocking. I wanted to confront Arthur right when he had some other woman . . . Well, I opened the door and went in."

"And did you kill Arthur Cushing?" Judge Norwood asked. "Now, understand me, Miss Keats, you don't have to answer that question, you are not forced to. You don't have to incriminate yourself. You . . ."

"Of course I didn't kill him. Why should I kill him? I

loved him. I took one look at what was in that room and let out a scream that Nora heard as plain as day. I dropped the compact, turned and ran out of the house. Nora can bear me out in everything I say. She knows I didn't shoot him. She heard the scream; she didn't hear any shot.

"By the time I got back Nora had moved over to the driver's seat. I simply jumped in the car and said, 'Get away from here quick, Nora. He's dead. Someone has shot him, the window's been smashed, and there's broken glass all over the floor.' "

Mason said quietly, "I think, Your Honor, I have no further questions."

"No further questions?" Judge Norwood said. "It seems to me there should be lots of questions. Apparently there has been a suppression of evidence and a conspiracy of silence. . . . Mr. Lansing!"

"Yes, Your Honor."

"Did you know anything about this?"

"I can assure Your Honor I am so completely bewildered and surprised I cannot get my mind oriented to these new developments even now."

"Mr. Hale, did you know anything about it?"

"Naturally not, Your Honor."

"Well, you know about it now," Judge Norwood snapped.

"Yes, Your Honor."

The judge turned to Marion Keats. "Miss Keats, you *could* be telling the truth. On the other hand, I suppose you realize that if the revolver was in the glove compartment of that car, as Carlotta Adrian claims, there was every opportunity for you to have taken possession of that revolver, recognized the fact that there was an excellent opportunity to commit a crime which would avenge you upon the decedent, and at the same time fix the blame on your rival, that you took the compact in one hand, the gun in the other, went to the house and . . ."

"But I didn't, Your Honor."

"I am stating that there is every opportunity for you to have done so. Do you realize that?"

"Well, I suppose . . . yes."

"You don't have to answer questions that are going to incriminate you," Judge Norwood said, "but I am going to ask you whether you opened the glove compartment of that car."

"We . . . We had every reason to believe that Carlotta Adrian . . ."

"I am asking you whether you opened the glove compartment of that car."

She raised her head, looked the Judge in the eyes and said, "Yes, we did. We went through that car with a fine-tooth comb. And there wasn't any gun in the glove compartment. It had been thrown out even then. It . . ."

"Just a moment," Lansing interrupted with his harsh, husky voice. "I am not accustomed to practicing criminal law, as the Court well knows. However, I am mindful of my position and my responsibilities in the matter, and due to circumstances which have come as a great surprise to me, I now find myself in the position of representing a witness who may be charged with crime. I am, therefore, advising you, Miss Keats, not to answer any more questions."

"You and your advice!" she stormed. "*You're* the one who got me into this."

"Just a moment," Lansing said. "I am warning you, Miss Keats, as your attorney, that you are not to answer any more questions. You are to refuse to make any statement on the ground that anything you may say may tend to incriminate you. Now, I suggest that you leave the witness stand."

"That's the first good advice you've given me," she said, hurrying down past the lawyers and to the crowded courtroom.

Judge Norwood pounded with his gavel. "And I, in turn," he said, "will suggest to the sheriff that this woman should be taken into custody until there can be further investigation. In the meantime the Court is going to take a recess and I am going to ask Counsel to join me in my chambers."

Judge Norwood arose from the bench and walked rapidly to his chambers.

Mason waited for Hale to join him, but the district attorney, engaged in a whispered conference with Ives, managed to avoid Mason's eye.

Mason strolled into Judge Norwood's chambers, and a moment later Lansing entered, then District Attorney Hale, then C. Creston Ives.

"I want you to understand I knew nothing of this, Judge," Lansing said. "I . . ."

"I'm quite certain you didn't, George," Judge Norwood reassured him.

"I tried to tell you last night but you wouldn't listen," Mason said.

Lansing shifted his position and became very uncomfortable.

"If you'd listened," Mason went on, "you might have spared your client a lot of unnecessary grief."

"Unnecessary?" Judge Norwood asked. "Good heavens, Mr. Mason, you can't . . ."

"Unnecessary," Mason said. "She didn't kill him."

"Mr. Mason, are you aware that you are making a peculiar and rather dangerous statement? You are still attorney for Mrs. Belle Adrian. In the event Marion Keats didn't kill him, then Carlotta Adrian did and your client is an accessory."

"What makes you think that?" Mason asked.

"Because there were only two people who entered that house after Carlotta Adrian departed. We now know that one of them was Marion Keats and I think it is pretty obvious from the evidence that the other one was Belle Adrian.

"Now, if Marion Keats is really telling the truth it is quite apparent that Carlotta Adrian must have been the one who killed him, that she went home and told her mother, and her mother went over there for the purpose of removing evidence, which makes her an accessory. . . . It has to be one way or the other."

"No, it doesn't," Mason said, and grinned as he saw Judge Norwood's face flush.

"Look at the evidence," Mason said. "It is now quite apparent that whatever the reason that actuated Belle Adrian in going over to that house, after she got there, she started cleaning up. Both Sam Burris and his wife saw her moving around as though she were cleaning things up, and it's quite evident that she picked up the compact knowing that it was Carlotta's, took it home and hid it in a shoe."

"That's what I've been telling you," Judge Norwood said. "What are you trying to do? Crucify your own client?"

"I'm merely pointing out that since Arthur Cushing couldn't stand up on his foot, since he had a servant to do all the dishes, that it is quite obvious he wouldn't have been washing dishes."

"What in the world *are* you talking about?" Darwin Hale asked.

"I am pointing out," Mason said, "that when Mrs. Adrian entered the place, found Cushing dead, found a highball glass with lipstick on it, she naturally assumed that her daughter's fingerprints would be on that glass. So she very carefully washed and polished it and put it in the cupboard."

Judge Norwood frowned. "I am not certain I follow you, Mr. Mason."

"Don't you get it?" Mason said. "There was one glass smashed on the floor in the midst of all the broken glass. That was the only glass there. The other had been washed and polished by Mrs. Adrian."

"So what?" District Attorney Hale said. "You're taking up a lot of our time at a most important and crucial moment with a lot of extraneous comments, Mr. Mason."

Mason met his eyes. "If you think it's extraneous, just start figuring it out. Perhaps you'll want to read a transcript of the testimony. You fellows ganged up on me here with the idea of accusing me of abusing the process of the court, so I'm damned if I'm going to do *all* your thinking for you."

Judge Norwood suddenly sat bolt upright in his chair.

"Good heavens, Mr. Mason, you can't possibly mean that the evidence of that glass indicates that . . . ?"

"I do," Mason said.

Hale looked at Lansing, then at Ives, then at the Judge. "I don't get it," he said.

"You will," Mason told him. "In time."

And with that the lawyer calmly walked out of the Judge's chambers, pulling the door closed behind him.

Chapter 21

Back in the hotel, Paul Drake and Della Street entered the suite with Perry Mason.

"Gosh," Mason said, wiping his forehead, "I thought I'd never get through that crowd of reporters yelling to know what was happening."

"Well," Della Street asked, "what *is* happening?"

"I can't tell," Mason said, looking at his watch, "but I think probably within the next fifteen or twenty minutes those guys will have unscrambled the puzzle."

"You mean you didn't unscramble it for them?" Drake asked.

"Hell, no," Mason said. "I gave them a hint and walked out."

"Why didn't you give them the whole thing?" Drake asked.

"Then," Mason said, "I would have been the high-priced city lawyer trying to sell them a bill of goods and they would have been suspicious. As it is, I'll let them figure it for themselves and by that time they'll have sold themselves on it as their idea. It'll be their baby."

"Are you sure you gave them enough so they'll get it?" Della Street asked.

"Judge Norwood got it," Mason said.

"Just what did he get?" Drake inquired.

Mason said, "There are three sets of tracks to Cushing's cottage, and one set of tracks leaving the cottage."

"You mean Carlotta's?"

"That's right."

"Of course, Carlotta could have killed him. She's now the logical suspect, and . . ."

"No, she isn't. Start looking the thing over. It shows complete premeditation and deliberation. That glass was smashed deliberately and for a purpose. Nobody threw the mirror at Arthur Cushing, and Arthur Cushing didn't throw the mirror at anyone."

"Well, why was it smashed?"

"For two reasons," Mason said. "One of them was to give the murderer a piece of glass that he could put in Carlotta Adrian's front tire so it would look as though she must have left the place after the glass was smashed. The other reason was to make noise enough so Sam Burris could state that he had been aroused by the crash of breaking glass and the sound of a shot."

"What are you talking about?" Drake asked. "Sam Burris?"

"That's right," Mason said, "the murderer."

"Are you crazy? He couldn't have gone over there without leaving tracks."

"Well, he left tracks, didn't he?"

"When he went over there after the sound of the shot, after the woman had screamed, after . . ."

"How do you know it was after the shot was fired?"

"Well, wasn't it? His wife says it was. It has to be."

Mason shook his head. "Sometime Saturday afternoon, Sam Burris had got hold of that antique mirror from the garage and smashed it up. While Carlotta was having her tête-à-tête with Arthur Cushing, Burris unscrewed the valve stem, let about two-thirds of the air out of her front tire, took his knife, cut a place in the rubber tread and inserted this long sliver of glass so that with the tire as flat as it was, the glass would be sure to perforate the tube. Then he took the gun out of her glove compartment and waited, at a safe distance.

"He did that early in the evening.

"By the time Carlotta left, the frost had formed. Burris walked up to the house carrying a sack full of broken glass. He killed Cushing, smashed the window, smashed the glass from the framed picture, smashed the glass that Cushing had been drinking from, spilled powdered glass all over the room, walked out, went home, waited half an hour or so and then wakened his wife, to tell her that he had *just* heard the sound of breaking glass. At about that time he began to get the breaks. A woman actually did scream. Then Mrs. Adrian showed up. . . . It only remained for Sam Burris to carry out his plan by claiming he was going over to investigate. He went out of his house and waited in the garage for ten minutes. Then he came back and told his wife he was going to have to go get the sheriff. He jumped in the car, drove down the road to where he found Carlotta's automobile stalled, and, without getting out of his own car, tossed the gun into the weeds; then he went and got the sheriff."

"But how do you know all this?" Drake asked. "How can you prove it?"

"Simply because when Sam Burris described what he found when he walked into that room he mentioned that there was a glass with lipstick on it. Then he realized what he'd done almost as soon as he'd said it, and tried to work in an explanation casually so it would appear he'd been talking about the bloodstained tumbler fragments on the floor.

"After you've cross-examined as many witnesses as I have you learn to recognize these symptoms of trying to cover up a slip.

"When I saw Sam Burris begin to resort to that same old cover up, I pricked up my ears, and then I began to do a *lot* of thinking.

"There actually *was* a glass on the table when Sam had *left* the room, but that was the glass with lipstick on it that Mrs. Adrian washed, polished and put away in the pantry. If Burris had been telling the truth he would have said he hadn't seen any glass on the table. He thought it was there right up to the time he let the statement slip out. Then he realized Mrs. Adrian must have been cleaning up, and would have washed the glass. So he started to cover up and showed all the typical signs of a cover up.

"Judge Norwood's got it," Mason went on. "The others will get it, after a while."

He stretched, yawned and grinned. "Okay," he said, "the case is over. Let's pack up and get back to town. I don't want to see the peaceful countryside for another six months."

"And that's all you had to go on?" Drake asked. "Just that slip on cross-examination?"

"Gosh, no," Mason said, "that was what started me thinking, and once I started to think along those lines, everything pointed to the real murderer."

"I don't get it," Drake said.

"In the first place," Mason pointed out, "Burris knew a lot about tracking. He admitted that on the witness stand, and as a man who had spent all of his life in this country he certainly knew that when the hoarfrost started to form it would show tracks. He *knew* that Mrs. Adrian had been over to that cabin. Therefore, he simply must have known that her tracks were there in the frost and with the coming of daylight could be followed with the greatest of ease.

"Yet, despite that fact, we find him going to Mrs. Adrian's home at just about daylight and advising her not to say a word about having been over to the cottage—under the circumstances the most foolish thing she could possibly do, and something that was absolutely certain to direct suspicion to her.

"Then we find him implanting in Mrs. Adrian's mind the definite feeling that Carlotta actually did commit the murder, knowing that Mrs. Adrian would do anything to protect Carlotta.

"Remember that the murderer's whole scheme had been to direct suspicion to Carlotta. Having done all that, Burris made a great grandstand play by pretending that he was trying to protect Carlotta, and her mother, thereby, of course, indicating that since the murderer had tried to frame the crime on Carlotta, Burris' attempts to divert suspicion from them would indicate he *couldn't* be the murderer.

"He was pretty cunning—the sort of ingenious cunning that a woodsman uses in trapping animals."

"But *why* did he do it?" Drake asked.

"Good Lord," Mason said, "he had all the motive in the world. He hated Arthur Cushing with a bitter hatred.

"Up to the time Cushing demonstrated the value of the Burris farm as a resort property, Burris regarded it only as fair-to-middling farm land.

"Then Cushing got an option on a choice site for a resort hotel, and not only that but got a long-term option on all the balance of Burris' holdings.

"Cushing could take up the option at any time at the contract price. Burris was stuck with the taxes and, of course, once the property became resort property the taxes were bound to go up to such an extent that it would break Burris just to pay those taxes.

"Once the deal became known Burris would have been the laughing stock of the community. Therefore, he hated Arthur Cushing with the bitter hatred of a man who has spent much of his time in an isolated community away from any broadening human contacts. And, of course, he had every reason to believe that since the entire scheme was Arthur's and since the elder Cushing would have no particular reason to want to make more money after his sole heir had been removed, it seemed to Burris that the murder of Arthur Cushing offered him the best way out.

"He felt Cushing would forget about the option, decide not to put up the resort hotel and withdraw from Bear Valley, whereupon Burris would have a free hand to interest some other promoter, this time on a more business-like basis.

"You have to take into consideration the type of mind with which we were dealing and the background. It's this type of mind that starts the bloody feuds. When people like Burris feel they have been wronged they start to kill. Burris lacked the courage and the plain guts to go out and shoot Arthur Cushing down. He resorted to cunning rather than courage, and when he knew, as most of the town did, that Carlotta was carrying Harvey Delano's revolver in the glove compartment of her automobile, he saw his opportunity. . . . Come on, let's get packed and get started before people start swarming in with congratulations, asking for explanations and trying to bum free legal advice. . . . The place for a lawyer at a time like this is his office."